I0549926

Murder and Homicide VIII

Peter J. Michael

Murder and Homicide VIII

Copyright © 2025 by Peter J. Michael
All rights reserved. No part of this book may be reproduced or transmitted in any form or by any means, without prior written permission from the author.

This is a work of fiction. Names, characters, businesses, places, events and incidents are either the products of the author's imagination or used in a fictitious manner. Any resemblance to actual persons, living or dead, or actual events is purely coincidental.

ISBN-13: 978-1-7640978-4-0

Published by Peter J. Michael

ALL BOOKS BY THIS AUTHOR ARE:

THE GREAT WAR AGAINST
TERRORISM

KILLING THE BOGEYMAN I & II

RUTHLESS

RELIGIOUS DEATH TRAP

THE GOD OF ELIMINATION

THE MURDEROUS MR. A

MADMAN'S RETURN

MURDER AND HOMICIDE I - VIII

Part 'eight' of the Murder and Homicide cops versus villains' fiction book series.

Murder and Homicide VIII

MURDER AND HOMICIDE VIII

CHAPTER 1

Robert Stewart felt the earth moving under his feet. At first, he wondered if New York City was experiencing an earthquake? It was 6:00 AM in the morning and Robert Stewart headed to the 25th division precinct station house of Brooklyn, New York front doors. He was walking briskly along the concrete path to the front doors of the police station, when he felt the ground vibrating under his feet.

At first there was just the feeling of movement, as if New York City was being struck by a natural disaster. But was that really the case? It wasn't until only a matter of moments later, that distant sounds in the background remotely nearby and oddly far-off from him made sense to what terrible feeling of movement he was experiencing beneath his feet.

Suddenly largely volatile, intense, fierce, heavy and ferocious sounds erupted from far and nearby. It started with one deep and terrible explosive sound. Then numerous explosive and destructive deafening sounds were heard in the distance, mixed with the sight of rising ash and red flames rising towards the sky. And that made perfect sense to Robert Stewart of what exactly was going on, that caused the intensely powerful and potently dangerous movement beneath his feet.

Some horrible person or people out there in the city had set off and detonated numerous lethal bombs that morning, to all explode at the same time on specific targets. And that caused the earth to move under his feet in a stormy and violent fashion!

It wasn't an earthquake. It was the detonation of numerous powerful-and-deadly bombs erupting by the orders of one horrible maniac within the vicinity of New York City, who had unleashed a terrible vendetta against specific targets that morning, to eliminate such targets and buildings all at the same time, in order to avoid any police intervention of the mastermind's plan to mark and kill his victims at once, most certainly 'all' concurrently simultaneously, without leaving a pattern for police to trace or identify beforehand, if the terribly destructive and murderous incidences were committed one after the other at different time intervals.

The mastermind behind these bombings intended to eliminate all his marked targets and/or their properties, businesses and homes, at the same time, so no one, no law enforcement officer, was given any warning prior the bombings' detonations taking place, in order to prevent the termination of all targeted individuals and targeted properties to be claimed at once, all together.

Robert Stewart pulled out his mobile phone from inside his navy-blue coloured casual jacket pocket. But he did not even need to dial any digits to his 24-hour posted officers out in the field. Captain John McCallum was the first who contacted him. Captain John McCallum was leading specific patrols in the Brooklyn area when he contacted Robert Stewart only moments after the bombings detonated and filled Robert in on exactly what was going on.

He informed Robert that the bombs targeted buildings of exactly 37 General Practitioner (GP) Medical clinics all over the city. But even though the detonations were destructive to properties and buildings, at least the GP clinics were blown up fortunately at a time when it was so early in the morning, that no patient or doctor was inside the premises. But, still, that only amounted to a small and temporary comfort. Because the police captain still had further bad news to confirm. John McCallum most certainly and without hesitation had some further bad news to report. Apparently, just as the bombs were being detonated across dozens of GP clinics across the entire city of New York, also masked gunmen were spotted breaking inside the houses of 50 GP doctors at the same time across the city and holding machine guns and large knives. The diabolically bloodthirsty assassins had used knives to stab and machine guns to shoot at the GP doctors and blow them away.

The assassins had killed 50 GP doctors inside their homes, by firing machine guns and stabbing them multiple times with knives, at the same time the GP clinics were targeted for bomb detonations across the city at this early morning.

The police who apprehended the assassins were embroiled in a heavily enmeshed gun battle against the numerous killers spotted across the city limits where the destructions and killings were taking place. The well-equipped mass murderers began shooting at police and police retaliated by firing their weapons at them, which resulted in half a dozen assassins being shot to death and the remainder making an abrupt escape and departure to safety at present. But the police were combing the entire city in a fervent chase to hunt each of the mass killers down one by one or altogether.

Captain John McCallum also informed Commander Robert Stewart that just as the doctors were eliminated, so too were their vehicles also blown up shortly afterwards parked inside driveways or garages located inside their residences, and the doctors' wives and husbands and spouses and children were also targeted by the gunmen inside their houses. All killed! All dead! Not only were the GP doctors executed at the same time inside their houses, but the doctors' families and loved ones were also cold-bloodedly murdered and brutally slain all systematically. The GPs across the city and state of New York who were located by the numerous gunmen inside their private homes and residences, all had their lives claimed at once, immediately, and at the same time. The very moment the mass killers kicked down doors and forced themselves brutally and monstrously inside the medical practitioners' residences, such doctors' houses at that time immediately and abruptly became an evil and wicked slaughterhouse trap!

Robert Stewart now understood what was going on. Robert Stewart was even able to point a finger at the mastermind behind this as he cursed the hideous and monstrously cruel, cold-and-calculated name of Armando, Armando, Armando. Robert Stewart knew it was Domenico Armando who was behind this. But the question this time was why? Why was that hideous sick-and-twisted maniac targeting medical practitioners? Why was he targeting doctors now and eliminating their families as well?

Just as Robert's mind was trying to finagle the puzzle to the motive of Domenico Armando's current terrorist attacks on doctors and their loved ones throughout New York City, Robert Stewart also had a sudden realisation, a brainstorm of who the next target was. The US Health and Human Services Secretary was currently on vacation in New York City. He was presently residing in a hotel in Manhattan. A very expensive hotel. Very prestigious.

Robert Stewart thought things through clearly in his mind. The situation was extremely serious at present, very severe. The present circumstances were gravely dangerous with mass murderous consequences, if it wasn't contained rather swiftly, cleverly, using or outmatching the mastermind enemy's cunning against him! So, bearing all that in mind, Robert Stewart's brain was running ragged thoughts at present.

NOW, if Domenico Armando was targeting doctors, that meant that he was also gunning for the US Health and Human Services Chief. That was exactly Robert Stewart's conclusion at this very point in time!

Robert Stewart quickly ordered Captain John McCallum to go and find the US Health and Human Services Secretary and pick him up and bring him to his police station office immediately, at once! On the double! Even if they had to arrest him and force him downtown to the police station, Robert Stewart clearly and bluntly ordered Captain John McCallum, "then you go ahead and arrest him. But you bring him to my office immediately down at police headquarters! **Because he's the next target for Domenico Armando's hitmen!!!** So, you go and find him and bring him to the 25th division precinct station house using whatever means of force necessary, if it comes down to that!"

CHAPTER 2

Captain John McCallum and Officer Paul Stewart made tracks to the very expensive hotel room in Manhattan being occupied at present by the US Health and Human Services Secretary. The two police officers arrived at the scene of the high-ranked government politician's Manhattan holiday stay very promptly. The US Health and Human Services Secretary was named Bill Parks. He was a 62-year-old man of American descent. He had salt-and-pepper thin, slightly balding hair, and was rather largely built in body structure and frame. His attitude also left a lot to be desired.

Bill Parks was not alone inside his hotel room. He had security detail planted on him comprising of the US Marshals. Captain John McCallum and Officer Paul Stewart provided their police identifications to the security detail outside the politician's hotel room, who showed them inside and allowed them entrance.

But Bill Parks insisted that his security detail remain outside his hotel room maintaining security and watch over his safety, also securing his privacy, as Bill Parks was not alone inside his hotel room this early morning. In fact, Bill Parks enjoyed extramarital activities behind his wife's back. Bill Parks was currently occupied in bed with a local hooker both naked inside the bedroom, fondling each other's bodies, as they both lay on the bed. Bill Parks kept complaining to the hooker of his wife's smelly vagina. Bill Parks had certain fetishes and sexual desires that his wife could no longer fulfil. She wasn't the sweet-tasting piece of fruit he married 15 years ago. But Bill Parks considered this hooker to be rather tasty and her juices rather savoury.

The hooker was a redhead 25-year-old sexy dame with great large perfect breasts and attractive facial and nicely shaped body curves, the US Health Secretary had strongly favoured. Bill Parks enjoyed experiencing his sexual fantasies with this lovely hooker named Foxy. Bill Parks nicknamed her, in poetic rhyme, Foxy Roxy, because he was able to get his rocks off with her, as he could no longer get his rocks off with his wife. He was currently sucking her tits and fingering her clitoris. And Bill Parks paid her handsomely, rather perfectly, for an extra perfect blowjob he wanted her to pleasure him with. And she replied as she took the extra-large sum of cash as happy payment from his hands, she placed on top of the bedside table beside her, "whatever you say Mr. Secretary!"

Bill Parks was relaxing on the bed as he fondled her body and tasted her with delight. He wanted to kiss her from top to bottom and completely all over. And then after she gave him a blowjob, he wanted to bang her hard in his favourite sexual position being doggy style sex. In himself he didn't care what she liked. He was paying for it, so he would indulge in his fantasies regardless of whether she enjoyed it or not, full stop. Bill Parks was as ferociously greedy and selfishly narcissistic with Foxy Roxy, as he was in heading his political post and political affiliations in the Republican Party as chief of the nation's healthcare portfolios.

Bill Parks was as self-serving in indulging his sexual fantasies with Foxy Roxy, as he was self-seeking in running his political juncture as healthcare chief to the nation's constituents. He outlandishly served his political profession as callously and uncaringly as the two words defined in their complete and utter hideous meanings, full stop!

Right now, Bill Parks was receiving his blowjob from Foxy. And after the blowjob, he looked forward to fucking her doggy style. As he banged her doggy style, he would place his hands on her beautifully shaped buttocks, and then stretch forward and place both hands squeezing those perfectly formed soft big breasts of hers many times, as he pounded his below-average sized shaft into her vagina, the same way a dog entertained himself sexually.

It wasn't long thereafter, when it was time for his well-timed doggy style sexual positioning. So, as Bill Parks pounded her from behind with violent thrusts of his erect penis inside her lovely vagina, he began smiling and then laughing in thoughts he voiced to her at the same time, as he penetrated her roughly. He basically admitted rather deliberately to his selfishness and his selfish stance in politics, as he said to her whilst banging her hard, "this is the life! This is what I work for. I spend the whole time lying, cheating and stealing all day as US Health and Human Services Chief, so I can get paid the big bucks and come here and fuck my favourite lady, Foxy Roxy. And you Foxy Roxy certainly get my rocks off. So, in order to see you, I have to work hard for my money - lying, cheating and stealing every day of my political career, now running the portfolio, I've been entrusted to safeguard, being the health of every constituent in the United States of America. Which I certainly never do safeguard their interests but my own and my millionaire-and-billionaire corporate mates!" He laughed and smiled and then smiled and laughed once more.

"Would you like to repeat that down at police headquarters!" Barked the strong voice of Captain John McCallum, who barged inside the hotel room through the open door of the corrupt politician's bedroom, overhearing his equally corrupt admissions in running his highly ranked post in the US Government of Washington, D.C. much like a dog's arse.

Both Bill Parks and his hooker girl named Foxy became startled at the police officer's and appearing, two police officers' surprised presence, and invasion of their personal privacy, who just witnessed their sexual rendezvous together, in addition to the lawmen's eavesdropping on the US Health and Human Services Secretary's diabolical admissions of selfishness and corruption, whilst serving his post high up in government, just to amass big bucks at the expense and deliberate neglect of people's healthcare needs, rather diabolically and hypocritically.

Bill Parks quickly stopped fucking Foxy and rather embarrassed at the police catching them both naked together, he tried to hide his male sexual anatomy (external genital system), by placing his hands around his erect penis at the same time, as Foxy used one arm to cover her breasts and the other hand to cover her vagina.

As Bill Parks recovered from his embarrassment in a speedily fast night-and-day transformative turn, and rapidly switched his bitter emotions to immediate anger, he spoke furiously to the two police officers present inside the room and said, "what the hell are you stupid bastard police doing here invading my privacy like this?" He now faced the two police officers, Captain John McCallum and Officer Paul Stewart, whom both extended their police badges to him and insisted that the security detail allowed them inside.

"We've come here to get you!" Ordered Captain John McCallum.

Bill Parks was very sore right now and quite angry in his response, "what the hell are you on about? What do you mean get me? I'll get you police; you don't get me. What the hell is all this crap about, you dumb policemen!"

It was at this point when Officer Paul Stewart lost his cool and didn't appreciate idiots large or small giving him or any police officer stupid lip. Paul Stewart immediately burst his words forward at the worthless insult of a US Health and Human Services Chief very bluntly and devoid of tact. "Don't be smart with us dickhead!" Officer Paul Stewart ordered savagely. "We aren't here to socialise with you. If you want to be smart with us, we will be smart with you, OK, smartarse. Now, listen here Loverboy. Get your fat arse off the bed and get dressed, because you're coming with us right now! And tell your hooker friend as well to follow the same orders, only in regard to getting dressed!" Officer Paul Stewart then turned to the startled and frozen hooker named Foxy and reiterated his words then directly to her. "Listen here sweetheart. Are you deaf? Get off the bed, get dressed and take a hike. Get the hell out of here and don't come back. We're not here for you. We're here for your friend Bill Parks!"

The yet startled hooker Foxy did as she was told. She jumped off the bed without even greeting a goodbye to the man who just paid her handsomely to give him a very sensual sexual service - and she walked to the nearby dresser and grabbed her clothing from on top of it, quickly dressed herself and exited the hotel room and the entire five-star hotel quickly without a word.

Bill Parks's hotel room was on the 28th floor of the thirty in total number of floors of the grand New York City hotel. And the two police officers present, also ordered Bill Parks to get dressed, which he did momentarily. Bill Parks again asked what this was all about?

Captain John McCallum hinted, "we believe there is a contract out on your life. So, you have to come with us before the people who are after you find you!"

Bill Parks seemed quite shocked and unnerved by this revelation. "What the hell are you people talking about? Why would anyone put a contract on my life? Why does anyone want me dead? This is bullshit, fucking horseshit. What are you two idiots on about?" He asked menacingly in a nuisance-like fashion.

Officer Paul Stewart lost his temper once again. He had absolutely no tolerance for shitheads and arseholes large or small, low-ranked or high-ranked people being smart with him or any member of the police force. "Now I've just had enough of you Bill Parks. Now that you're dressed, get your dumb arse in gear - and get yourself on the elevator. Because we're leaving this place and you're coming with us right now, voluntarily. Or you're gonna leave this place in one of two ways. Either we arrest you, force and drag you kicking and screaming the hell out of here, or we leave you here for the hitman to come and get you. And we instead drag your dumb arrogant arse out of this place in a body bag. So, make your damn choice. Come with us or stay here and die!"

It wasn't long before Captain John McCallum and Officer Paul Stewart convinced the sorry excuse of a US Health and Human Services Secretary to tag along for the ride inside their unmarked police car. And they were swiftly on their way to the 25th division precinct station house in Brooklyn, to meet face to face with the famous Police Commander Robert Stewart!

CHAPTER 3

As soon as the miserable excuse of the United States Health Services Chief was summoned inside Robert Stewart's station house office by Captain John McCallum and Officer Paul Stewart, Commander Robert Stewart forced him to take a seat in front of his desk, as the ground rules of his new destiny would be dictated to him quite severely. Because the terms of his existence at present were extremely strict - and Bill Parks was ordered to abide by those rules and conditions whether he liked it or not! For that reason, as of right now, the United States Health Services Secretary was most certainly forced into the hands of police protection. When Robert would explain that his life was hanging by a thread by the world's most monstrously brutal and diabolical tyrant alive today, evilly roaming the streets of this earth, who not only possessed the devil's luck, but in fact the person who was after Bill Parks right now, most definitely made the devil in hell, who floated the world, appear as a simple low-calibre snake, in comparison to the extremely powerful and extremely dangerous deadly maniac, who was gunning for the life and miserable fraudulent existence of Bill Parks at this present point in time!

Just as Robert Stewart was to explain the ground rules and all the delicate intricacies involved in the current fate and destiny faced by Bill Parks, Robert Stewart was briefly but unhelped, distracted, by the desk sergeant who stormed his office seeming rather surprised, when he notified Robert, that he just received a phone call from a man who identified himself as Domenico Armando, wanting him to patch through his call to Robert Stewart's private landline office phone.

Robert Stewart ordered the desk sergeant to put him through. Robert insisted that he would take the call. The desk sergeant alerted Robert that the phone call was on line 3 extension - and Robert also insisted the desk sergeant to record the phone call and attempt to trace the telephone call at the same time. But Robert knew Domenico Armando would be using a secure phone and a secure phone line, and that trace location would be too diverse, leading them to false localities around the world and likely dead ends. But nonetheless, Robert Stewart asked the desk sergeant to put him through.

So just as the desk sergeant left the office, Robert Stewart picked up his landline phone receiver on his office desk and punched in the correct line 3 numeric extension with his finger and quickly took the call.

Commander Robert Stewart immediately identified himself through the phone, and shortly thereafter his caller identified himself deliberately and fervently as Domenico Armando. And Domenico Armando was calculated and intentional in his communications this time with his arch-enemy rival and number one staunchest enemy Commander Robert Stewart. No pretences. No disguised voice. And no shields whatsoever to his identity. Domenico Armando was straight to the point, cold-bloodedly purposeful, intentional and ferocious in every word spoken to his staunchest enemy and cunning nemesis Robert Stewart!

Domenico Armando's tone of voice was rather harsh, hostile, angry, even fiercely savage, with violent connotations, as he firmly insisted to Robert why the hell did he remove that scum US Health and Human Services Secretary Bill Parks from his Manhattan hotel room earlier that morning - and deprive him of the pleasure from sending his people to eliminate him! Perhaps it was a crazy question he directed to Robert Stewart. But still, he directed the question anyway, out of extreme hostile anger and vengeful fury! Domenico Armando's terrible wrath was very much apparent during this razor-sharp powerful conversation he directed towards Robert Stewart at present!

Robert Stewart's instincts were correct yet again! It was Domenico Armando responsible for the mass slaughterhouse killings of 50 GP doctors and their families - and the explosively destructive powerful bomb detonations of 37 GP clinics being blown up around New York City that morning. Robert Stewart was certainly right again! Domenico Armando was behind this mass destructive, and mass murderous rampage committed this morning within the perimeters of New York City and New York State.

Robert Stewart firmly responded to the horrible and brutal tyrant's question with equal seriousness, frankness, without beating around the bush. "Simply to prevent your evil hands from getting to him first and doing away with him, just as you killed all those GPs and their families, blowing up the numerous GP clinics in New York's perimeters all at the same time, earlier today this morning."

Domenico Armando seemed very angry. "I want that bastard dead! That fucking piece of shit deserves to die, that fucking scum! You know what he did? Do you know, do you have any idea what evil atrocity that fucking scum worthless insult of a US Health Services Secretary was guilty of committing? You know the atrocity? Do you have any idea about the true extent of the unconscionable wickedness that sonofabitch has committed, both him and all the corrupt doctors that he is legitimising their corruption, and criminal actions in medicine, as US Health and Human Services Chief? That fucking cunt Bill Parks has been responsible for killing my son! My secret son that no one knew about! The great son of my offspring is now dead! 'George the Great' is what I called him. He was only 21 years old. And he died from what the doctors called a mysterious illness.

"Everything is mysterious to those fraudulent fucking GP doctors and every fucking doctor that exists in this world and in this city, because they are frauds and ignorant scoundrel, diabolically evil and wicked cunts! They all are guilty of murder and mass murder! Every scum medical practitioner in this country and in this world intentionally kill their patients by their ill-knowledgeable training and lack of morals and ethics and human decency in practising medicine - and carrying out their medical duties properly and correctly towards their patients. **Or should I say, their 'victim patients!!!'**

"Those fucking pig scumbag despicable and disgusting doctors are the most fraudulently wicked legalised criminals in this whole world! They get paid to torture, torment, destroy and kill their patients for large sums of money. They are slobs and terrorists! Their medicines are ineffective or lethal! And that fucking scum US Health and Human Services Secretary Bill Parks had kept the health system in this country outrageously corrupt, as others before him had done so for years and decades!

"That scum Bill Parks is amongst the most wicked and evil, sick and sadistic coward politician in Washington, that the United States has ever seen. That scumbag piece of shit Bill Parks is practising evil and wickedness in Washington, D.C., the capital city and federal district of the United States of America, inside his high-ranked government post in charge of this country's entire healthcare system! So that's why that despicable walking atrocity piece of trash and insignificant piece of garbage, whose name is Bill Parks, truly deserves to die for all the horror and terror he has unleashed in the medical community in this country, which had been responsible for causing millions of patients in this entire nation to suffer and to die at the same time, as losing their money to corrupt heinously criminal doctors, who do nothing for them-those patients who see them, but destroy their health and steal their money! So that's why I want Bill Parks dead.

"And you Robert Stewart have deprived me of that pleasure, that justice; my revenge for the death of my son, that that fucking scum piece of shit worm of the ground, useless, worthless cunt Bill Parks was responsible for killing, my wonderful and handsome son George the Great!

"Bill Parks deserves to die, just as all those doctors in this city and this country. You see my friend Robert Stewart, I eliminated those stupid GP doctors earlier this morning, and I also eliminated their families, because those fucking doctors were responsible for killing my son who was a golden child of my family! OF MINE!!! What I did to those GPs and their fucking families was simply justice! It was poetic justice!

"And that scum Bill Parks behind all this medical corruption in this nation, did everything he could to undermine patients' treatments throughout this entire country. He made medical treatments unaffordable. The cost of prescription drugs is through the roof, the most expensive in the world under that scum Bill Parks autonomy as United States healthcare chief! Medical insurance premiums is unaffordable for most people. And that scum Bill Parks only intends to compound the suffering of doctors' patients, by planning to double and triple, yes, he wants to ultimately triple the cost of medical insurance premiums monthly, so nobody can afford to be treated for anything, in hopes that they all die.

"And those scum doctors are all worthless frauds anyway. Even if someone could afford to see them, the doctors do not care to treat their patients correctly. They give them medicines that kill them. They misdiagnose patients' illnesses, which causes patients' diseases and health conditions to drastically deteriorate and worsen to lethal proportions very quickly, which costs them-the victim patients their lives, as it had most certainly cost the life of my wonderful son recently, called George the Great!

"And the scum behind all this corruption is the US Health and Human Services Secretary called Bill Parks. That scum. That fucking useless and worthless scum, who is nothing but a fucking sewer rat piece of shit, lowest form of garbage, who does not deserve to live and breathe for one second longer! He was behind all these atrocities and medical corruption which exists at present in this country. That walking calamity Bill Parks is responsible for killing millions of people, as he surely and most certainly had been responsible for killing my son George the Great only recently!

"That fucking worthless rat, useless cunt Bill Parks doesn't deserve to be breathing! He deserves to die! He must suffer and suffer royally! And you Robert Stewart... Huh, you Robert Stewart, had prevented me from unleashing my justice against that fucking scum Bill Parks, who was the one truly behind my son's death! Bill Parks is running a criminal racket in the medical community, that is causing millions of people to be disadvantaged and eventually die, from a lack of healthcare and a lack of proper treatment by callously evil and wicked doctors; such evil disaster areas called doctors, who are overpopulating this entire country.

"And you... You Robert Stewart had been responsible for breaking my heart this day. You should not have taken that scum from his Manhattan hotel room. I had orchestrated a plan to make sure that Bill Parks's hotel room in Manhattan was his death trap. And you Robert Stewart foiled my plan. Bill Parks is an evil and wicked scumbag criminal politician. He is one of the worst and most disgusting filthy maggot pig politicians that the United States of America has ever seen. That scum Bill Parks should be suffering right now. I wanted to torture him. I wanted to make him scream the very tortures of the damned before he died! But before he died, I wanted him to bark like the fucking dog that he is. I wanted him to suffer for every crime he was guilty of committing inside his highly ranked government role! I wanted him to be cut in pieces, for the cold-and-calculated brutal slaughter and unconscionably unmerciful diabolically devious and shrewdly cunning, money-grabbing murder of my great son George.

"But... But... You robbed me of my justice Robert Stewart. You robbed me of my revenge Robert Stewart! You hurt me terribly this day Robert Stewart. And for that, I will get revenge against everyone who robbed me of my justice in killing Bill Parks this fucking day!

"You Robert Stewart are going to pay for what you have done! Because make no mistake about it my friend Robert Stewart, one way or another, I will eventually get my hands on that fucking piece of shit worthless worm of the ground filthy pig, motherfucking cunt, useless worthless shithead Bill Parks - and I am going to rip and tear all his body parts off his entire body. And I am going to rip off his fucking head, for what he had done, the brutal cold-and-calculated evil monstrous murder of my son George the Great! And you Robert Stewart will not get in my way. Because right now, I declare war against you Robert Stewart! This is a fucking war between us Robert Stewart that I declare as of right now! Right fucking now, we are at war together! You want to protect that scum Bill Parks? Well, we will see if you are able to really prevent me from eliminating him! Because eliminating him I will do! And you Robert Stewart are not going to stop me. You might have slowed me down right now in my plans of justice against that fucking worthless insult of a US Health and Human Services Chief. But in no way, no fucking way, have you prevented my justice from eventually being unleashed against that fucking worm of the ground scum, who goes by the name of Bill Parks!

"Because Bill Parks is going to die! Bill Parks is going to suffer! I will slaughter that worthless worm of the ground. Because he has been responsible for torturing and tormenting millions of sick people throughout the United States of America. And at the same time as Bill Parks was responsible for offering the poor in this country unaffordable healthcare costs, and wickedly evil, grossly deficient proper-and-correct medical assistance, via his directed fraudulent neglect throughout the United States of America, he also was responsible for stealing patients' monies at the same time, as he legislated evil policies for evil medical practitioners to torture, torment and steal the money of their patients. And all of the combination of such evils in this nation's health care system, resulted in eventually killing those patients through that ineffectiveness of poorly executed and deliberately incorrect medical treatments, delivered together with the callously evil wickedness of prescribing lethal medications, deadly drug medications from deadly drug companies in this country! And let me tell you something my friend Commander Robert Stewart: **Everyone is going to pay for that!!!** Every medical practitioner fraud and evil practising doctor is going to suffer for what they have done, the brutal and callous murder of my great son George! Everyone is going to pay! Everyone will fucking die for that! And you Robert Stewart are in for the fight, the fucking war of your life! Because I'm going to get Bill Parks and you… You Robert Stewart are not going to fucking stop me! You will see. Yes, Sir! You will see! You will see! You will fucking see my friend Robert Stewart!!!

"Because let me fill you in on the entire story about my son George the Great! You see, before my son died, he sent me a letter stating the terms of his funeral he wanted me to carry out for him. He didn't want a conventional burial. Because he didn't want people to witness via an open coffin, how that horrible disease that he had, had reduced his good looks and made him look extremely terrible. So, because he didn't want people to see him looking as bad as the disease he suffered from made him look, he insisted that as soon as he died, his corpse be cremated to ashes. So, I did as he wished. And I kept the ashes of my precious son's corpse in my possession. I carry his ashes with me inside a colourful glass vase with his cremation ashes inside.

"Whenever possible, I keep this vase of my son's cremation ashes by my side at all times, in memory of my great son George; I carry his ashes by my side at all times, as a constant reminder to me of what the fraudulent doctors and what that fraudulent scum pig Bill Parks had done; the atrocity they 'all' committed against my son. Which was the cold-and-calculated slaughter of my son George. But first they tortured my son. They misdiagnosed him and let his health condition rapidly deteriorate to the point where my son became embarrassed and ashamed of what his disease made him look like. He didn't want people seeing him. He didn't want people to witness his horrible transformation, from the most handsome man, reduced to becoming one of the most repulsive. And that's what he described himself to be in the letter he sent to me just brief moments before his death.

"And the people responsible for his medical decline and death, are the scum doctors in our medical community throughout this country. And the fucking piece of shit behind it all, was that motherfucking scumbag cunt Bill Parks. It was Bill Parks who legislated evil policies to evil doctors, to wickedly destroy their patients - and never offer them any hope of recovery from their illnesses whatsoever!!! It was Bill Parks behind the current healthcare system in the United States of America being in utter turmoil, devastating shambles, and a complete catastrophe, which does nothing but cause excruciating destruction and painful deaths for millions of their patients throughout this country. And that is something that Bill Parks will never get away with. I want Bill Parks incinerated. I want Bill Parks tortured and killed! I want that fucking cunt Bill Parks to be tormented, as he tormented my son with evil legislative policies, that caused evil fraud and stealing throughout the medical community in this country. And that horrendous corruption of monumental proportions, which currently resides in the medical community, surely and definitely resulted in my wonderful son George the Great's death sentence, at the hands of wicked and evil, and thieving medical practitioners throughout this country - and throughout this fucking world. Those scum doctors study falsehoods and rubbish in university. Their teachers are fraudulent and criminal teachers of scams, untruths, dishonesty and fucking falsehoods. Just like the students of medicine they teach and graduate to become doctors, the teachers are all scum. **Scum! You hear me? SCUM!!! Yes, they are all fucking scum!!! Scum! Scum! Fucking scum!!!** That is why I have always been against teachers. Because they teach their students, such as those fucking cunt doctors responsible for killing my son, **'lies and rubbish',** which results in the torture and destruction of all their victim patients!

"That fucking fat slob, overweight fat bum, bulky-and-slimy pig, Bill Parks, is filling his belly, with the wages he is getting in his high-ranked government profession in Washington, serving as this country's US Health and Human Services Secretary, for doing a grossly evil job. That greedy thieving stealing, criminally uncaring swine Bill Parks, is eating hearty meals, whilst everyone else in this country, millions and millions of people, most people in this country, are simply starving to death, living on starvation wages, unable to keep their heads above water. And that fucking piece of shit Bill Parks is laughing at all this. He is a sadistic cunt, who is laughing at all the misery of millions of people in this country he's inflicting such horrendous suffering against! He gets paid very handsomely, and in return for those wages, that he is stealing for doing an absolutely incompetent-wicked job, he is deliberately serving his role, his post in high office, not only fraudulently and negligently, but, he is serving his post and his role in high office in Washington, D.C., wickedly and evilly, intentionally depriving the sick, the dying and those about to be dead in this country, of proper medical care! That is what that scumbag sewer rat Bill Parks is guilty of performing in his job every day of his miserably pathetic, destructive and horrendously criminal life as this country's Health Secretary. That is the scum that you protected from his well-deserved death. That piece of shit deserves to die.

"And that is the scum that you deprived me of the greatest pleasure from eliminating this day. And that my friend Robert Stewart is not justice. What you did was a complete injustice to me and my family name. An injustice to my dead son, George the Great! And many people are going to pay for that injustice! From the smallest of those worthless doctors in this country, those worthless scum doctors operating in this country - to the largest pig of them all, who has legislated evil, wicked, sick and destructive policies in the United States of America, which resulted in medical corruption to be at the levels of epidemic proportions; which has also resulted in the deaths of millions of doctors' patients - and the horrendous brutal torture, evil suffering and shocking death of my wonderful son, George the Great! And for that my friend Robert Stewart, many people are going to pay for that death, that injustice of my son's death of George the Great!!! And no one will suffer more than that fucking pig scumbag Bill Parks, who is behind all this corruption!

"So, protect him well Robert Stewart. Because your efforts to protect that scumbag will all be in vain. Because eventually, I am going to get my hands on that fucking worthless worm of the ground. And I am going to tear him apart. I am going to spill his blood. And he is going to pay, pay, pay, fucking pay, for the death and destruction of my wonderful handsome son George the Great!!!

"Yes. Those fucking doctors in this country are not well-trained. They are certainly not well-trained at all. But instead, they are all frauds! They are all frauds, just like the criminal teachers in university who trained them! And that's the cause, that's what the US Health and Human Services Secretary Bill Parks is legislating. That miserable worthless scum Bill Parks is behind all this medical corruption committed by doctors in this country. Bill Parks is allowing those evil corrupt doctors to get away with misdiagnosing patients' illnesses, and thus in turn, because of such misdiagnoses and deliberate neglect, the doctors are always getting away with in fact killing their patients. Just like they killed my son George the Great at the very very tender age of 21!

"That scum Bill Parks behind all this medical corruption in this country, truly deserves to die for the cold-and-calculated, ruthless and brutal murder of my son George. And you stopped me, Robert Stewart. I'm very angry at you Robert, for depriving me of the pleasure of killing that fucking scumbag sonofabitch worthless, useless fucking cunt Bill Parks!

"I wanted him dead! He deserves to die for being responsible for killing my son George the Great! Both him and all the doctors in this world, in this city of New York are all corrupt! Every day they are killing their patients and getting away with it. And that's been because of that worthless sadistic evil cunt US Health and Human Services Secretary Bill Parks, who is legislating his corrupt policies, which allowed doctors to get away with killing and murdering their patients by the millions, just as they were responsible for misdiagnosing and killing my son George the Great!

"My son George died only two days ago from an illness he kept from me, until only just before his death. My son George was a strong, healthy and handsome prince of a son to me! And because of the doctors' fraudulent practises and ignorant and criminal negligence in the field of medicine, they did nothing to help my son, when he rapidly became very ill! And he was diagnosed by my own doctor only when it was too late. Because my son was so embarrassed of his condition and how it transformed him from handsome to sickness, which stripped him of his flesh, and made his handsome looks become terribly grotesque. My son looked terrible in the end. And all the flesh and muscles of his body was wasted away, and reduced to skin and bone. So, my son hid himself from the world. He lived a recluse. And would not even face me or my doctors to seek help. He was embarrassed and humiliated with how his declining health condition made him look, from the most handsome man in the world, to one of the ugliest, he described himself and his transformation in the letter, he sent to me before his death!

"He had a terrible neurological condition which destroyed him. You see, doctors are so stupid, they know nothing about the nervous system. They cannot diagnose and they cannot treat anything. Can they fix cancer? No! Can they treat or fix any brain condition or physical condition whatsoever? No! Those doctors are complete fucking frauds. Ignorant scum, who learned nothing but trash at university, taught by trash teachers. That's the doctors we have, complete liars and ignorant stupid bastards and bitches, who know and understand nothing about the human anatomy. They know nothing about treating anybody, no matter what disease they have - mental or physical. The doctors know nothing about any human condition. They do not know how to treat any human medical sickness, disease or condition. They do not know how to diagnose any human sicknesses, by means of understanding the intricate truths, and possessing the relevant knowledge and knowhow, to fully comprehend what causes people to become mentally and/or physically ill, full stop!

"Those doctors are complete frauds. In fact, calling them frauds is a fucking understatement!!!

"And because of all this medical corruption, my son George's health condition deteriorated rapidly. And his illness eventually destroyed him. Because the doctors deliberately, through their negligence and corruption, misdiagnosed him and mistreated him, causing my son to become deprived of proper medical care throughout the course of his very excruciating and horrendous illness. And as a consequence of this despicable and disgusting medical condition, whose origins were of a neurological nature, his deterioration was inevitable. And his certain death thereafter was imminent!

"And because of the doctors' evil and wicked ways in practising their diabolical brand of medicine throughout this world, that alone, had caused my son's health condition to drastically and rapidly decline. And without proper medical doctors, who possessed proper medical knowledge, mixed together with doctors' lack of morals and ethics, together with an absence of decent character, and the scarcity of caring, thus lacking the legitimate desire to cure their patients, all resulted in my son George the Great's unfortunate and tragic demise! My son became so weak in the end, that his heart gave out. And because of his extremely serious medical condition not properly treated by all those scum doctors out there in this world, his heart was unable to function properly due to the exhaustion of his neurological condition - and he shortly collapsed onto the floor of his bedroom, experiencing heart failure. His heart stopped just as quickly as the click of a finger, when he eventually died! He died at the very young age of 21!

"And because of that unfortunate and senseless death, which could have been prevented, if any medical practitioner in this world was truly worth even a single penny in terms of brains and character, that was the fundamental reason and reasons why I… why I wanted revenge. My beautiful retribution against that fucking scum Bill Parks, behind all this medical corruption that exists in this country today!

"And YOU Robert Stewart deprived me of that right. You Commander Robert Stewart deprived me of that pleasure and justice that I deserved, that my son deserves for his death and his senseless slaughter, in which that fucking worthless insult of a Health Services Chief, Bill Parks, was responsible for legislating such medical corrupt policies in this country, which, in turn, killed my son!!! And those evil policies of Bill Parks, were certainly responsible for killing my son! That scumbag Bill Parks was truly behind my wonderful son, George the Great's death!

"You deprived me of my pleasure, of my fucking right for justice and retribution against that scum Bill Parks, who was behind all the medical corruption in this country! You, Robert, took that scum from his Manhattan hotel room. And you took him into your custody, to protect him; to protect that worthless piece of shit, who does not deserve to live!

"Do you expect me to be happy about that Robert Stewart? Do you expect that I'm going to let you get away with that? Because one way or another, I am going to get that fucking cunt Bill Parks!!! So, you can try to protect him. You can try with all your fucking might! But let me tell you something my friend Robert Stewart: **Your powers are limited compared to my powers!** I have more power, resources and manpower than you can ever dream of accumulating against me. So, bear that in mind! And understand that very salient truth of what you are really up against!

"And you had better also understand the repercussions of that truth are as follows: when I say that I want Bill Parks dead, dead is exactly how he will become! And you understand one very important fact, another very important truth, my friend Robert Stewart: **You will not stand in my way!** So now, this is the game plan… You can try and hide that scum Bill Parks from me - but I will eventually find him! And I will slaughter him. And I don't give a fuck, and I don't give a damn, about what you have to say about it! Because whatever attempts you make to protect him, I will foil those attempts, with my equal-and-greater fervent actions, to slaughter that bumbling idiot and criminal fraud Bill Parks, for the death of my wonderful son… my now dead son, George the Great!

"So, get ready Robert Stewart for the fight of your fucking life! Because I am going to get that scum Bill Parks and you will not get in my way. I promise you that, my enemy Robert Stewart!!!" Domenico Armando shouted evil-mindedly, with nefariously villainous intent, mixed together with destructive, hateful, malicious and vile unpleasant ugliness, embedded throughout his entire demeanour, as he instantly that moment hung up the phone on Robert's face.

Without any delay, Robert Stewart then turned to Bill Parks and faced him dead on in the eye. Robert Stewart quickly verified to Bill Parks that Domenico Armando who just telephoned him, confirmed that he was after him-Bill Parks, and was gunning for his life.

Furthermore, Robert Stewart informed the US Health and Human Services Secretary Bill Parks, that right now, he had no choice but to stay put and remain in police protection! Because if he did not, Bill Parks was a certified dead man!!!

CHAPTER 4

Robert Stewart explained to Bill Parks that he would be taken to a safe place in the city, until all the paperwork was completed and arrangements for his departure out of the country was safely underway.

It was no state secret or hush-hush cloak-and-dagger private and concealed unacknowledged fact and truth to the entire country as a whole, that Bill Parks was horrible at his job, and his choice to resign from federal government serving as Health and Human Services Secretary should be **'effective immediately!'** It was also not mysterious, confidential, hidden, secluded, clandestine or confidential, that since he came to office most recently after the Republicans won the election, he ran his role as the nation's Health Secretary much like a disaster! And as a consequence of his grubby hands playing sick and wicked games on every portfolio of the health care system throughout the entire country of the United States of America, it resulted in a very short time frame, a very dire outcome, which had certainly placed the entire health system of the entire nation collapsing quite rapidly into the ground.

In a nutshell, Bill Parks was absolutely shit at his job! He instantly made quick changes to portfolios, that proved to disadvantage millions and millions of poor and working-class citizens across the entire United States of America. Not to mention that the sudden withdrawal of government support and closures of very important government services, which ordinarily, would assist the sick, the dying and those very close to death itself, as necessary for their lives remaining amongst the living; when such medically ill and financially impoverished people, had been struck with very, very serious health conditions and life-threatening illnesses; such necessary health portfolios and government-funded health programs being stripped to the bone from them; that miserable outcome certainly resulted in such disadvantaged poor citizens of the country having to fend for themselves. And eventually face the consequences that their critical and severe health conditions left unaffordable at present, unable to be treated under the Bill Parks Nationwide Healthcare disastrous policies of rip and tear, neglect and corruption as it were, since his extremely unfortunate appointment to that role of nation's Health

Chief, quite recently, would result in such sick patients' very rapid and sudden deaths!

And based on all that fiasco, chaos, incompetently disastrous horror story, mixed together in one toxically bad ingredient after another, resulting in one divisive and destructive fucking scandalous and infuriating shitshow imposed onto the health care system across the entire United States of America, at present, by Bill Parks, the resignation of the current sitting nation's Health Services Secretary, should instinctively and most certainly, become, simply put, a fait accompli!

Thus, taking into consideration such damning facts of all that ruinous evidence thrown into his face in tantalising humiliation and present-day damnatory community uproar, the outcome of removing himself from office should come quite naturally!

Therefore, given that decision by the nation's proven dangerously unstable, chaotically disastrous, dementedly toxic and calamitously devastating Health Secretary, Mr. Bill Parks, of absolute and certain resignation from serving in any capacity inside federal government ever again, Mr. Bill Parks, would consequently be placed in permanent protective custody, being given a fake name and phoney credentials, to forever live in a secret location abroad! And his wife would join him as the only living tie to him in the country. Bill Parks and his wife possessed no children, and no other living blood relative close by to consider their safeties, so there was nothing else to worry about on that end!

CHAPTER 5

Robert Stewart laid it on the line, all the gory details, for the abruptly exiting federal politician and his post as Health and Human Services Secretary Bill Parks, to comprehend his calamitous state of affairs at present in a very grim and dark reality.

"So, Domenico Armando really wants to kill me?" Asked the soon-to-be, ex-federal politician of the United States of America Bill Parks, wearing a rather cool façade, as he asked that very dangerous and deadly serious question to the cool-eyed police commander.

Robert Stewart saw through the mask facade that Bill Parks was wearing in front of him, as he was seated in front of his desk, and Robert Stewart stood aside him, cementing the facts, with no debating on the reality of the soon-to-be ex-Health and Human Services Secretary Bill Parks's grim reality he currently dealt with.

Robert Stewart immediately tore through the mask of his rather cool emotions protruding on the surface, and studied the true petrified hidden expression on the face of Bill Parks, when Robert Stewart replied to the question by stating in reference to Domenico Armando gunning for his life: "that's as sure as hell!"

Bill Parks broke out a yellow smile at that confirmation to his question being forthrightly answered and said, yet maintaining his cool façade, "Speaking of hell, I've got quite a fascinating story I would reveal to you shortly about that particular subject, Commander Robert Stewart!"

Robert Stewart replied only on the subject concerning Bill Parks's life being in grave danger by Domenico Armando at the same time as appearing to ignore Bill Parks's current statement. "Domenico Armando went to great lengths this morning to settle many in his mind, sadistic personal scores. He wiped out many, what he described as, corrupt medical doctors across the city and state of New York. And now Domenico Armando is machinegunning for you as we speak, Mr. Bill Parks. Because he blames you as responsible for all the medical corruption in this country that cost him his son, he names George. So right now, we have to take you to a temporary hiding place in this city, until permanent arrangements can be made for you to exit this country completely and never come back! And right now my officers are going to be risking their lives to protect you, until federal authorities can collect you into their custody and escort you under armed guard, to take you personally to a private plane in New York, that will fly you to a secret location abroad, so Domenico Armando will never be able to find you and never be able to make good on his threat on your life!"

"It sounds like it's been one hell of a rough morning!" Responded Bill Parks.

"It's only bound to get rougher!" Exclaimed Commander Robert Stewart. As he explained furthermore, "Domenico Armando is a bloodthirsty killer. And he's not going to stop until he finds you and makes good on his promise to kill you. So, until your elaborate transport out of this country, you'll be in our custody. And we the police are going to make sure that this temporary hidden location of yours in New York is as impenetrable as a fortress. Because you can bet one thing: wherever we take you, Domenico Armando will not stop looking for you. He's going to send his people to attempt hits on your life - and all of us police officers will be caught in the middle of that. Domenico Armando is a master homicidal maniac. And he is determined to find you and destroy you, because he blames you as responsible and behind New York City's medical corruption that cost him his son George's life! And whilst you are here in this city, he is going to send professional killers, professional hitmen to find you and to eliminate you! And that's where we come in. The job of the police is to prevent and to stop any such attacks on your life no matter the cost! So meanwhile everything will be closed down and securely guarded around you. Every exit and entrance to your personal whereabouts will be blocked from any outsider! Every door and every window will be covered. We will have officers patrolling the entire street of your hiding place you will be taken to. And the entire city will be covered by round-the-clock surveilling policemen and policewomen. That will include helicopters, police sniffer dogs, heavily armed police covering inside and outside your temporary location inside this city - and your wife is also under heavy guard until you will be reunited with her on the private plane ride to your secret location overseas, so Domenico Armando will never be able to find you!"

Bill Parks seemed preoccupied in sombre thought at present at the mentioning of his wife. "I'm sure she will be devastated that she has to leave her life in the United States of America as First Lady and be forced to live overseas in hiding so abruptly. I'm sure she will be crying and no doubt blaming me for all this!"

Robert Stewart replied, "well, she will come to understand the necessity of all decisions concerning yours and her departure from this country. She will be made to understand why it has to happen this way. Because just as Domenico Armando is after you, we believe Domenico Armando will also be gunning for your wife. Reason being, this morning Domenico Armando committed a mass murderous slaughterhouse group of cold-blooded killings against New York City's medical practitioners. Domenico Armando executed approximately 50 GP doctors who were killed in a series of machine gun bullets and brutal stabbings. Also, and at the same time as those killings took place, Domenico Armando had orchestrated the brutal mass slaughters of more people. He was behind the assassinations of their entire families, their wives, their husbands and their children. That is why we believe Domenico Armando will be after your wife as well. Fortunately, you don't have any children to worry about. Because if you or your wife had any children in your marriage or previous marriages, they would also be joining the two of you abroad in safe custody.

"Now, since Domenico Armando had managed to order the brutal executions of GPs and their entire families inside their homes this morning, we are absolutely certain that Domenico Armando is not only after you, but he will also be after your wife as well. Because in Domenico Armando's very sick and twisted mind, he believes that you were responsible for all the bad policies in this country which resulted in the death of his son.

"Domenico Armando is quit bluntly accusing you of killing his family, meaning, his son George. So as a result of Domenico Armando's lunacy and retributive actions, he's not only going to be after you Mr. Bill Parks, but he will also be gunning for your wife. He will most definitely be going after your wife. And since he blames you for killing his son through bad policy initiatives which caused corruption in this country's healthcare system, I repeat, he's going to kill your family. Meaning your wife. I also repeat those reasons why: as he blames you for killing his family, meaning his son George.

"Fortunately, for their sake, I must reiterate, you don't have any children. Because I can guarantee you if you or your wife had any children, they would also be made targets for assassination by Master Criminal Domenico Armando. So until you and your wife are safely on that private plane and that plane is airborne, high up in the sky, undetected by Armando or his people, every precaution to prevent Domenico Armando and his people from coming near you or your wife, will be taken by heavily-armed police groups, who are currently assigned to make sure that Domenico Armando never gets anywhere near the two of you!"

Bill Parks felt an eerie frightened chill surging through his entire body from head to foot at present. The thought of that master sadistic dictator, that brutally vicious and heartlessly cruel, merciless genius tyrant Domenico Armando's extreme determination to kill him, had definitely sent shivers through his spine and his entire body right now.

Bill Parks thought of Robert Stewart's words concerning Domenico Armando blaming him for his son George's death because of his very poor decisions as Healthcare Chief of the United States of America. Bill Parks knew he was guilty. Bill Parks kept that guilt to himself for now. But eventually the fear overwhelming his entire body would have him openly admit his guilt to

Robert, before he and his wife were taken out of the country permanently this afternoon.

Bill Parks knew that Domenico Armando was dead on the money when he blamed him as Health and Human Services Secretary, being behind the current turmoil and trouble, corruption and destruction, that faced America's current health system. Bill Parks knew he had to take responsibility, because he simply didn't give a damn about doing his job properly. After all, in himself, Bill Parks had money, he had power, he had prestige, and he had position. But given all that, his selfishness and greed still forced him to make horrendous errors of judgement, and quite deliberately, against his fellow constituents throughout the United States of America.

He only cared about his own personal health care requirements and wealth-driven affordability to doctors if need be. He suddenly came to the realisation only when it was all too late for him, that he had seriously fucked up in office. He seriously fucked up! He fucked up! He fucked up! He did not give a fuck about the little guy, about the hundreds of millions of what he considered little insignificant people in the United States of America. He didn't give a fuck about their health care needs or whether they could afford to go and see a doctor, or whether they could afford to purchase their extremely high-priced prescription drugs needed to prolong their lives.

Bill Parks knew he was selfish. Bill Parks knew he didn't give a damn about serving his constituents correctly. Bill Parks only cared about serving himself and the money his position as health chief of this nation would grant him in his role, inside the federal government of Washington, D.C. Bill Parks only cared about the big bucks he made inside the White House as nationwide health secretary. And to hell with everybody else and their health care needs. But it only dawned on him now, that his uncaring attitude had suddenly brought very bad and very serious karma against him. **And that karma was called Domenico Armando!**

Because Domenico Armando at this very moment, wanted to unleash justice against Bill Parks. A very diabolically evil type of justice! And the only thing that was between Domenico Armando and Bill Parks was Robert Stewart and his army of New York City Police Department Law Officers!

In himself, Bill Parks could only wonder if Robert Stewart actually gave a damn about saving his life. And quite often during his present struggles, he wondered to himself whether Robert Stewart thought such things. Whether Robert Stewart perhaps believed inside his very secretive mindset that Bill Parks deserved to die.

But that aside, Robert Stewart was just doing his job! Whether Robert Stewart thought that Bill Parks deserved to die because he was a horrible man and a horrible uncaring unconscionably evil and wicked politician was not really taken into consideration at present. The reality was still relevant. Robert Stewart naturally had opinions on matters as any other law enforcement officer, even just the same as any civilian in society. But he kept his opinions to himself on that matter. Because on the subject of whether Bill Parks deserved to get exactly what was warranted, befitting his past actions and misdeeds, was still extremely relevant in his own mind. But Robert Stewart had a much greater foresight in mind at present. Because Robert Stewart was just doing his job in making sure that Domenico Armando or his people never got their hands on him, meaning Bill Parks!

So, Robert Stewart was basically doing everything within his power and position to stop Domenico Armando from killing Bill Parks as current health services chief of this nation, only to prove a point to himself, by frustrating his greatest enemy in the world Domenico Armando. And making sure that Domenico Armando did not get another bloody mass murderous notch in his belt, by successfully killing both Bill Parks and his targeted victim wife! And that was it. Full stop.

Whether Robert Stewart cared for the life of Bill Parks was irrelevant. Robert Stewart had a vendetta against Domenico Armando. Robert Stewart wanted Domenico Armando dead! Robert Stewart wanted to hunt Domenico Armando down and find him and kill him. That was the crux of it. And Robert Stewart would do everything within his power to make sure that Domenico Armando constantly failed in his sordid plans!

Meaning, that if he knew who Domenico Armando was gunning for, the target's identity, Robert Stewart would do everything within his power to make sure that Domenico Armando was unsuccessful in carrying out that hit, with additional reasons to frustrate Domenico Armando, as a personal vendetta against him, that seemed forever unending at present! Because Robert Stewart considered Domenico Armando to be his worst enemy in this entire world. Robert Stewart wanted to find Domenico Armando! And Robert Stewart certainly wanted to kill Domenico Armando! That was understandable!

Domenico Armando was a sick man, a very sick ruthless wicked and horrendously evil homicidal maniac, mass murdering son of a bitch bastard snake! In Robert's mind, Domenico Armando was not going to be successful in killing Bill Parks or his wife, because Robert Stewart wanted to make sure that no matter who the target was, Domenico Armando would come up goalless and empty-handed, falling short of achieving any sort of victory in carrying out that hit.

Robert Stewart was not only doing his job, but he had a personal vendetta against Domenico Armando. And he wanted Domenico Armando to be destroyed. Robert Stewart wanted Domenico Armando to be killed. Robert Stewart wanted in himself to kill Domenico Armando personally, full stop!

Robert Stewart wanted revenge! Robert Stewart wanted retribution! Robert Stewart wanted justice! Robert Stewart wanted poetic justice against his worst enemy in the world called Domenico Armando! And if part of that justice meant that Domenico was unsuccessful in carrying out his orders to kill Bill Parks which included his wife, then Robert Stewart would do everything within his power to stop and foil Domenico Armando's next victorious kill, which included Bill Parks and certainly his wife. And that was all Robert Stewart had to say or think on that score!

So as long as Bill Parks was in the city until his departure, Robert Stewart intended for him and his police troops not to let Bill Parks out of their sight for even one second. Because it would only take one second of distraction for Domenico Armando's assassin, one of those professional assassins he would send out gunning for Bill Parks's life, to successfully land their attempt on claiming the life of the current Health and Human Services Secretary of Washington, D.C.!

So, in his mind, in his heart and in his soul, Robert Stewart would do whatever necessary to make sure that Domenico Armando remained unceremonious in his hit against Bill Parks. And in turn, Robert Stewart would do whatever it took to nail Domenico, even if he had to turn the entire country upside down, he would do it. He would do whatever it took to locate and find Domenico Armando and put the final stake through him! Robert Stewart intended to drive the final stake into Domenico Armando's black wicked heart and render him defenceless, motionless and finally dead! Unable to rise again!

Because the game between Robert Stewart and Domenico Armando was a deadly chess game. It was a real-life chess game. Domenico Armando wanted to play a game of cat and mouse, full stop! But Robert Stewart had a different game in mind. It was still a chess game. But his brand of chess was strategy and victory for the New York City Police Department. Robert Stewart's brand of chess was to defeat and checkmate his target Domenico Armando. And Robert Stewart intended not to be disappointed in his outcome and masterful tactics of strategy in outmanoeuvring and outwitting, and outgunning and outplaying Domenico Armando, in their bloody warring chess game between them they currently faced against each other!

Domenico Armando, the sick sadistic monster he was, thought that he was going to bulldoze the police in his efforts to finally claim the life of Bill Parks and his wife. But in himself, Robert Stewart considered that Domenico Armando had another thing coming to him. All in all, Robert Stewart intended not only to stop Domenico Armando's killer army regime from getting anywhere near Bill Parks, but at the same time, Robert Stewart was strongly committed for him and his police troops to instead turn the guns on Domenico Armando's assassins - and slaughter them on sight, cold and deliberately, as soon as they were spotted coming anywhere near them or their target Bill Parks and their target's wife, for that matter!

Robert Stewart had numerous charges he wanted to lay out against Domenico Armando. There were numerous mass murder killings throughout his sick and destructive existence, that forced Robert Stewart to want to fire bullets into Domenico Armando's body as punishment for committing! And Robert Stewart was working for that day, when Domenico Armando would most certainly pay the piper and face the consequences, and be laid out in front of him, by his cunning investigations and cunning trap, he would set out for Domenico Armando. To basically lure him into his hands. Robert Stewart intended to smoke out Domenico Armando. To extract him from hiding, so that Robert Stewart could finally get his hands on him - and make him pay for all the mass murderous killings and mass carnages of bloody deaths, that Domenico Armando had been responsible for committing, throughout his entire sick and twisted existence on this earth!!!

Robert knew that for years, in fact for decades, Domenico Armando was trying to take over control of New York City. Domenico Armando wanted New York City in his pocket. Domenico Armando wanted to dominate New York as a whole and control every aspect of the entire city and state. He wanted to control every business, all the politicians, with undeniable and absolute political power, and he wanted to control the police. BUT Domenico Armando had one giant roadblock in his path. He always had to contend with one giant obstacle in his way of accomplishing his grand goals of absolute control of New York City and the United States of America. And that person who posed a severe and drastic roadblock against him was called Robert Stewart. Robert Stewart managed to outwit him on more than one occasion. And Domenico Armando was very bitter concerning that ruinous accomplishment against him, by the only person in the world who was able to penetrate his otherwise very impenetrable armour - and stop him cold on more than one occasion.

Domenico Armando considered Robert Stewart to be his ultimate adversary. His number one archenemy nemesis in this entire world, that no one else could ever come close to the cunning and dangerously clever scope that Robert Stewart possessed within his grasp, so expertly, and naturally, against the Armando Empire's Patriarch, Domenico Armando. And because of this strong and ruthless competition that Robert Stewart constantly had thrown Armando's way, Domenico Armando and Robert Stewart and Robert Stewart and Domenico Armando were destined by fate and destiny itself, to become sworn bitter rivals until the end of time!

Robert Stewart ascertained that Domenico Armando's maniacal ideological standpoint to even target police too, over power and control, was most certainly the blueprint to Domenico Armando's rapid destruction in the past and in the present. Robert Stewart considered that Domenico Armando blew it, he blew his entire world apart, the day he tried to outfight and outgun the police in their attempts to stop and neutralise the Armando dictator dead in his tracks!

Robert Stewart had already forecasted wild visions of Domenico Armando's obituary coming to reality in his mind. Robert Stewart wanted to dictate the very strict and lawful terms of Domenico Armando's farewell from not only New York City, but from the entire nation of the United States of America and the globe itself, at large, full stop!

Robert Stewart wanted to rid the entire world of Domenico Armando, not just New York City. And in himself, Robert Stewart would go to whatever lengths necessary and declare whatever war he had to, in order to accomplish the total destruction, absolute ruination, and complete termination of giant kingpin notorious madman and diabolical tyrant Domenico Armando!!!

Robert Stewart didn't want Domenico Armando just imprisoned for life. No! No! No! Robert Stewart wanted Domenico Armando terminated by the very law he tried to overthrow. Robert Stewart wanted that son of a bitch either on the electric chair or on the receiving end of his target practise officer's powerful gun and powerful bullets aimed at Armando's direction, and firing at him, a spray of brutalising and tormenting lethal showers of blood-spilling bullets, plunging into the entire body of Domenico Armando, until Domenico Armando collapsed onto the ground in front of him, unable to rise up again back from the dead.

In crux, Robert Stewart wanted Domenico Armando as dead as the countless victims Domenico Armando was responsible for claiming in his sick and twisted, evil and wicked reign, as the ultimate boss of bosses he thusly sealed such title and hierarchical stature and ultimate position in the underworld, throughout the grand scheme of things!

Robert Stewart understood that Domenico Armando's entire game strategy was divide and conquer. And that was the exact strategy Robert intended to use but against Domenico Armando and his evil Armando Family Empire.

Robert Stewart willed his strongly calculated goal to strip Domenico Armando of his power, by eliminating all his influence and manpower, thus dividing his empire into walls collapsing, and sending his entire kingdom crumbling to the ground in tatters. And to send his entire world blown sky-high around him, by dividing his empire through endless crackdowns and an elimination process of all his henchmen pawns.

Robert Stewart intended to conquer his bloody war against Domenico Armando in spectacular fashion! Robert Stewart planned, quite purposefully, to first finagle a stalemate against Domenico Armando, by crumbling his entire empire and removing his hideous armies of killer men - and stripping him of his money and resources at the same time. Then through that accomplishment, Domenico Armando would face a check on the chess board. And as soon as Robert Stewart got his hands on Domenico Armando, he intended that check to become a permanent checkmate victory of the final battle and final war, that he and Domenico Armando would play out in this real-life, lethal-and-dangerous, bloody-and-deadly chess game war between them.

But the war between them was not a chess game per se. It was not carried out in the same traditional rules as a chessboard. The game between Robert Stewart and Domenico Armando was real-life chess, utilising real-life strategies of policing against the underworld of arms against arms and death against death; and overthrow against overthrow, of all the opponents' manpower armies and lethal opposition, the Armando family in particular, posed against the proper powers of law and order throughout the United States of America and the world itself!!!

Robert Stewart was hunting big game! And that big game was called Domenico Armando. Robert Stewart wanted to defeat and demolish Domenico Armando's name, rank and serial number! And this time, Robert Stewart intended that, Domenico Armando was not going to get away with anything! Not a single crime he committed! And he would never get his evil and wicked hands on Bill Parks!

Robert Stewart in himself would do everything within his power to ensure that Domenico Armando never got to Bill Parks in any successful murder plot! Robert Stewart, however, was very self-assured and very satisfied in his thoughts, that Bill Parks was going to get exactly what he deserved, for being the country's most lousy health secretary that the United States of America had ever seen. Bill Parks would be stripped from his freedom to do what he wanted: to lie, to steal and cheat his way into office - and scam and victimise the constituents of this nation any further. Because Bill Parks was going to be isolated with no freedoms at his disposal. He had to lay low much like a prisoner. And remain hidden from the world for the rest of his life! And Robert Stewart considered that that was mighty justice for the sick crimes, scams and hideous conspiracies, that Bill Parks was guilty of committing, throughout his destructive and disgustingly wicked life as a high-ranked government chief, and one of the worst crooked politicians that this nation had ever witnessed in power and authority over anybody and anything. And that suffering contrived against Bill Parks, was a terrific justice against his evilness and wicked ways against this country and its people, Robert Stewart considered, wholeheartedly and justifiably!!!

So, I hope you are listening to my words and my thoughts Domenico Armando. Robert Stewart then thought to himself. Yes. Now I'm talking to you. Bill Parks is going to suffer my way. You are never going to have the personal satisfaction of clipping that extra victim under your belt. And then... then... Domenico Armando, I'm going to find you. Yes. I'm going to find you personally, and I'm going to nail you to the wall, you dirty bastard, for every act of wickedness and evil you have committed in your sick and destructive life on this earth. I hope you can telepathically read my thoughts and hear what I'm saying to you Domenico Armando. Because I am gunning for you! And I will eventually find you Domenico Armando. And when I do find you, prepare to be sent back where you came from, inside the gates of hell!!!

I'm going to use every resource at my disposal to destroy you completely Domenico Armando, for all the brutal mass murders you are guilty of committing, throughout your horrible days of planning and plotting, scheming and conspiring in the dark, as the diabolical snake and hideous demon from hell you truly are. That I promise you, Domenico Armando. If it is the last job I do here inside the New York City Police Department, I will nail you to the wall finally! I'm going to send you to hell Domenico Armando, to rot and burn there forever and ever! So, get ready, because I'm coming for you! **Your days of holding this city and country as hostages to your tyranny are numbered.** You are fast approaching a nightmarish end. Yes, Domenico Armando. I-me-Robert Stewart certainly have an obsessive disdain for you! And that disdain has your name on it! So don't you worry about anything Domenico Armando. You don't have to find anything! I will personally show you the way and escort you down the dark tunnel into the gates of hell myself!

You have fired your last gun, stabbed your final victim, and you have finished detonating your bombs on your final victim(s). Because the next bullet that's fired, and the next bomb that goes off, will be headed your way Domenico Armando. So, prepare to die Domenico Armando! Prepare for your destruction, because it is coming Domenico Armando and very, very soon! I'm going to put you on the spot Domenico Armando! Yes. I'm going to witness you Domenico Armando, the boss of bosses and head kingpin of all the international underworld rackets running scared. I want to see you scared Domenico Armando. I want to see the look of intense fright and terrible trauma in your eyes, as you know what's coming for you! Your death and destruction Domenico Armando is what is coming for you! So, I'll be ready for you right now.

Come and send your paid guns out for Bill Parks. But I promise you one thing, Domenico Armando, your attempts to claim another life especially under my watch will come up empty!

You said Domenico Armando that you consider me your greatest enemy. Because I'm the only man alive who knows as much about you as you know about yourself. I know that bothers you Domenico Armando. I know that really worries the hell out of you. And you know something Domenico Armando? It certainly should bother you. Because that's what I'm here for. I'm certainly not here to make you comfortable. I'm certainly not here to bring about peace in your sick life. No. No. Not at all. Quite the opposite, my murderous enemy! Indeed. I'm here to give you in return, what you gave to the world! I'm here serving in this police station to wreak havoc upon you and bother the hell out of you permanently, until your entire existence is removed from this earth!!!

CHAPTER 6

Robert Stewart studied the clear vision of fear in Bill Parks's eyes. Bill Parks was certainly experiencing a plentiful supply of fear, panic and paranoia at present, from the Armando Chief Domenico Armando's attempts to come after him and do him a very horrendously brutal justice for the murder of his son George. Yes. Domenico Armando classified his son George's death as a murder. And he clearly and obviously blamed Bill Parks as head of this country's healthcare portfolios, to the same degree, being the very man ultimately responsible for killing his sick, dying and finally confirmed dead son George.

So naturally, Bill Parks was petrified and shaking like a leaf at the thought of Domenico Armando getting his hands on him. Bill Parks knew about Robert Stewart's history. Bill Parks knew that Robert Stewart was the best cop in the business. But, at the same time, Bill Parks also knew about Domenico Armando's history. And understood that Domenico Armando was the worst criminal that currently lived in the United States of America, if not the world itself!

Robert Stewart was currently assigned to protect Bill Parks. And Domenico Armando took it upon himself to find, destroy and tear the guts out of Bill Parks, until Bill Parks was dead at his feet. This was simply another game of Who Will Win This War?

Would Robert Stewart outwit Domenico Armando's attempts to kill the healthcare secretary of the country, or would Domenico Armando outgun Robert Stewart and finally succeed in murdering Bill Parks, as the man he blamed truly responsible for the death of his much-loved son George? What a poetic game of chess this truly was, Bill Parks strongly considered. Two great chess players. Two brilliant gamesmen. And two brilliant minds. Robert Stewart and Domenico Armando pitted against each other for opposite reasons. One wanted to prevent the other from killing a politician, and the other attempting desperately to overpower all obstacles in his way, in order to kill this one politician who went by the name of Bill Parks! This game was sheer brilliance personified. Bill Parks took a breather from his worried thoughts to contemplate that brilliant game between two master strategists and master combatants, Robert Stewart and Domenico Armando. Each one trying to outmanoeuvre the other, with him, Bill Parks, in the middle of the ferocious warzone between those two wartime leaders.

Bill Parks almost smiled at the thought, until his depressed preoccupied thoughts and deep state of worry about being targeted by Domenico Armando, sent his constant anxiety-filled emotions into turmoil once again. As soon as he gathered his thoughts, he would be speaking and asking Robert Stewart some more questions.

Bill Parks hoped that he would be able to control his emotions and gather his thoughts any second now. But the growing worries, the growing fears, the growing anxieties and the growing depression that he was a target to the world's sickest and deadliest maniac, who went by the name of Domenico Armando, certainly unnerved the fucking hell out of him.

Bill Parks was scared shitless from Domenico Armando. Bill Parks was scared knowing that his life hung in the balance right now, and he was worried if Robert Stewart was really able to protect him and safely escort him on time to his private plane in the city, destined to leave this country once and for all, before Domenico Armando's goons were able to get their hands on him. These thoughts seriously unnerved him and caused a hell of a lot of troubled anxieties racing through his mind endlessly!

Bill Parks comprehended that Domenico Armando was a very sick and dangerously determined uncontrollable maniac; a complete lunatic running around the streets of this city somewhere anonymously. Somewhere hidden, but able to travel invisibly, much like a diabolical magician, that Domenico Armando was indeed known to be and become, when needed! And Bill Parks was immensely worried that Domenico Armando could get him anytime. He knew that even with Robert Stewart and the entire New York City Police Force protecting him, that Domenico Armando could still find a way to get him. Domenico Armando could use any form of artillery weapon or deadly item, to cause death and destruction on him and all those around him, as quickly as a diabolical magician's trick! Domenico Armando could use any means of lethal artillery and death-inflicting item to get to him.

Could Domenico Armando be planting a bomb somewhere? Could Domenico Armando be planting hidden killers out there within the streets of New York City waiting for him? Could Domenico Armando be planning to fly a plane in the sky over their heads and drop a powerful and destructive bomb to blow everybody up, including him? Maybe Domenico Armando might unleash some poison gas in the air and get to him that way! Maybe Domenico Armando might poison the entire city's water supply. Domenico Armando could get to him by any way and any means. Bill Parks was certainly not ignorant to Domenico Armando's criminally evil tactics and his unlimited potential in unleashing death upon someone, utilising the most dreadful and destructive methods. Domenico Armando's unique style, his entire sordid trademark and blueprint, which revealed an unlimited supply of resources and capabilities, in order to outlive his objectives and claim his victims, no matter who they were, or how hidden they were from society inside the world itself, were truly well known in many famous circles of law and order and all levels of government.

Bill Parks firmly understood that Domenico Armando was a man with a mission. And his means of accomplishing his missions had no bounds to them. And knowing that, Bill Parks began to sweat. He began to panic. Bill Parks began to shout in terror. His entire emotions were unleashed much like a thunderstorm, as his words finally came out of his mouth and he spoke to Robert Stewart in a mixture of fear, paranoia, terror and horror, when he said to Commander Robert Stewart this instant inside his police station office: "that bloody Domenico Armando cannot be allowed to get to me. But I fear that he will! And if Domenico Armando is able to get to me through you Robert Stewart, then I am dead!!!" He continued his thoughts verbally to the Police Commander Robert Stewart. Bill Parks said furthermore, "look at me Robert Stewart. What the hell is this miserable sight you see before you? I-Bill Parks, US Health and Human Services Chief, suddenly is running gutless. Bill Parks who was always a cool customer and ferocious in his demeanour, suddenly is running scared. I am running scared of the big bad wolf Domenico Armando coming after me, to finally kill me. What a shameful pathetic sight that is. I never thought I'd live the day to see myself reduced to fear and anxiety. What a horrendous transformation. Really this life is unpredictable. This world we live in can turn on someone without a moment's notice.

"One minute you can be confident that things are running your way, and within a blink of an eye, things can turn and make a strong man weakened to his knees; a secure man trembling in humiliating fear. Look at me. Just look at me. What a mess I have turned into. I never thought I'd live to see the day when my entire life would be reduced to rock bottom. I am being forced to run away and give up everything that I love, including my job. And I'm doing all this because there is a madman after me. A very sick madman. A twisted lunatic. I truly am a pathetic existence of a man! I'm truly ashamed of myself, Commander Robert Stewart. But to tell you the truth, I really did bring this on myself. I became a smartarse in my post in government. I became cocky and arrogant. I was selfish and inconsiderate. I looked down on the lower-class. And I went out of my way to ruin them with policies that certainly did divide this nation. I favoured the rich and I disadvantaged the poor. And now I guess, I'm paying the ultimate price for my actions of wickedness towards my fellow man.

"Now I'm reduced to experiencing the very same fear my policies had evoked towards millions and millions of people in this country I served, as their high-ranked political leader. I divided this nation, and my policies of subjugation placed one group of people against the other - and favoured the rich against the poor. I had penalised the poor for being poor. And suddenly I find my evil and wicked ways being turned around towards my face. Everything I did, all my hideous plans was for nothing! It all backfired. My policies caused fear and unnerved millions and millions of my fellow constituents throughout this country. And now I'm experiencing that very same fear I caused to so many millions of people, by the sheer 'Horror Story', the miserable truth, that the evil Domenico Armando is after me! What a horrendous thought. What a horrendous nightmarish reality my existence has transformed into.

"From Big Shot US Health and Human Services Chief, to now running scared. Big shot smart aleck Bill Parks all of a sudden turning gutless. Fucking hell, Commander Robert Stewart. Fucking hell, fucking hell, fucking hell. Life has a way of throwing things in people's faces. And I just got all the shit that I threw at this country's face, now thrown back in my face, in spades." He repeated yet again, "Fucking hell, fucking hell, fucking hell! I believe I'm truly fucked now. I'm really fucked!

"It was only this morning when I was in the bedroom of that Manhattan hotel with Foxy Roxy, that I thought I had the world at my fingertips. At least I thought I had the whole country's lifeblood hanging by a rope and being led by a leash. I thought I had everything under control firmly in the palm of my hands! I thought I was untouchable. Foxy

Roxy certainly made me feel untouchable. Now I will never see Foxy Roxy again. And I'll never be able to serve in any capacity in government again. And I'll never be able to step foot into this country again after this day is through. Either I'm going to leave this country by a plane or by a bullet.

"I fear it could be by a bullet. But I guess we'll wait and see. The exciting part about this is the game that you and Domenico Armando are playing together Commander Robert Stewart. This fantastic chess game between the two of you now revolves around me at present. One of you is working to prevent me from being killed and the other is possibly going to blow up the entire country in order to bring about my demise and murder! Only one of you will win this war! I'm just terrified with uncertainty of which one of you will turn out to be the winner in this big play being orchestrated here! Because if it is not you Commander Robert Stewart, I truly am what you declared me to be earlier, a certified dead man!!!

"Ahh, my life is fucked now! I guess that is the main story I wanted to tell you about hell earlier. All evildoers as I, me-myself are heading there. The thing is, all of us boneheads are just so clueless and stupid, that we never take that into consideration, or realise the truthfulness of that fate of ours, until it is all too late and we're already dead and thrown down there by force!

"Fucking hell, Commander. I'm just thinking about my life right now. It wasn't enough that I had a good paying job. It wasn't enough that I had Foxy Roxy by my side at my calling and payment. I had number one and number two. But I was a fucking greedy son of a bitch. I had to go for number three. And that was imposing my will and my devilish greed upon my constituents of this country. I had to force my hand stupidly. I had to play my hand foolishly, by changing portfolios in government rapidly and dividing the whole place up.

"And because I did all these terribly bad things, now I'm paying the piper for it all. Now I have the worst person in this world imaginable after my blood because of all my bad deeds. My misdeeds certainly have caught up with me. I mean for fuck's sake, I've got a fucking monster demon from hell, Domenico Armando out for my blood. Can it possibly get any fucking worse than that? I certainly don't fucking think so. I mean anyone else after me I'll shrug it off. But fucking hell, the fact of having this psychopathic sick maniac Domenico Armando after me, claiming that my bad policies as health care chief of the United

States of America was responsible for corrupting the entire medical system in this nation that cost him his son George, is not sitting very well with me right now, Robert Stewart.

"It's not sitting with me well at all, because I don't like being human target practise to one of the most dangerous and devilish dictators and wicked tyrants that this world has ever seen or created. And now this fucking bastard Domenico Armando is out for my blood. And to tell you the truth Commander Robert Stewart, I really have no one to blame for all this but myself.

"I wonder if only I could speak to the man Domenico Armando. Could it make a difference? If only I could apologise to him perhaps he might give me a pass!"

Robert Stewart shook his head briefly at this pitiful foolish display presented to him at present by Bill Parks. Robert Stewart suddenly spoke to him, but his words became a true testament that he was completely appalled at the literally denigrated ridiculous sight of a human being directed his way, as Robert Stewart insisted coldly to this foolish fraud of a politician before him, "Bill Parks, you are absolutely right to condemn yourself for your hideous actions as this country's healthcare secretary, whose policies were only designed to ruin most of the people in this nation. You are right to criticise and insult yourself over that. But the second part I heard you saying was not only completely ridiculous, but it was also shockingly stupid, to think that Domenico Armando would accept your apology and give you a pass for being this country's worst possible US Health and Human Services Secretary in its entire political history. You are very wrong to think that Domenico Armando would accept your apology. You are also very wrong to think that Domenico Armando would ever forgive you. You are wrong and stupid and utterly foolish and ridiculously dumb and contemptibly naïve and moronically clueless to think that Domenico Armando would give you a pass. Domenico Armando will only make your suffering all the more painful, before he brings you to your knees, scares you out of your wits, strikes terror into every fibre of your being and makes you shake in your shoes as he tortures every part of you from head to foot, until he finally renders you fucking lifeless!!!!" Robert Stewart exclaimed in powerfully realistic terms, at the same time as he was complete and utterly disgusted in this humiliating and embarrassing excuse of a, high-ranked United States political secretary, as Bill Parks once upon a time claimed himself to be. The CHIEF of the nation's health and wellbeing!

Bill Parks froze at the thought for a moment in complete terrified shock. At first, he was unable to utter any words. Then he composed himself and said, "So what you're saying is that I'm dead meat! Fucking hell, fucking hell, fucking hell. I'm a dead man. I'm fucking dead. I'm a Walking Dead Man! This whole security thing is a joke. I don't think anybody is able to protect me from what you're telling me. I don't believe anyone can protect me from the likes of that monstrous being called Domenico Armando.

"Domenico Armando is probably laughing at all of us, including you police. He's laughing because he knows anything you do to protect me Commander Robert Stewart will be an ineffectual failure! Just a disappointing non-success! Just a comedy of errors and blunders, because he will certainly and most definitely tear right through your police security and wipe me out, as quickly as you can say the words, 'bloody murder!'

"My life was pronounced over the second that maniac Domenico Armando decided to kill me. I don't believe I'm gonna walk out of New York City alive. I don't believe anyone can help me right now! I don't believe anyone can save me from his evil clutches! From the stories I've heard about Domenico Armando, this man is an invisible demon, who can virtually walk through walls. When he decides to kill someone, he kills them and no one, no force on earth, and no united group of armies the world can offer, no matter how powerful, can ever, ever stop him!"

Robert Stewart gave him a sarcastic smile. Then the police commander's face turned serious as he said confidently, "I wouldn't bet on that if I were you. Because it will be a losing bet. I guarantee you will lose all your money. One way or another, you're getting on that plane in New York City this afternoon, and you are leaving this country alive, both you and your wife! But meanwhile, you are going to be taken right now to protective custody, until the federal boys escort you on that plane this afternoon! So, as of now, this very moment, you're going to be taken to a secret place in this city, and we-the police are going to remain with you until the FBI and the SIA pick you up, and escort you using armed guards to your safe trip out of the United States of America permanently! So don't make any bets right now. Because you're leaving with us effective immediately!!!" Robert Stewart stated authoritatively, accepting no debates on the subject and no argument concerning the seriousness of all security precautions he would undertake, to ensure the safety of Bill Parks and his wife against the cruellest man alive in this world at present, known as Domenico Armando.

Robert Stewart would accept no sucker bet against his abilities to protect his subject from both Domenico Armando and his Armando family thugs! In Robert's mind, the police were not using boy scout tactics to protect Bill Parks or his wife, despite what that fool health services chief of this nation otherwise thought. Robert Stewart was going to use highly trained and extremely professional combative means of armed forces and tactical measures at his disposal, to prevent Domenico Armando from securing any form of victory in this very lethal-and-dangerous situation they faced at present!!!

CHAPTER 7

Robert Stewart escorted Bill Parks inside the top-secret safehouse located within the perimeters of New York with an army of police guarding every inch of the premises inside and outside.

The safehouse contained many rooms inside its five-storey building perimeters. And New York police were covering every floor, every door, every window, every entrance and every exit area of the entire building. There were police patrols flooding the entire street of the safehouse, keeping close watch for any Armando gunmen within the vicinity, attempting to approach the scene, as possible apprehenders of the whereabouts of their primary target at present called Bill Parks.

Robert Stewart would take every precaution necessary and security measure to ensure that Domenico Armando was unsuccessful in his plots for murder against Bill Parks and his wife.

Robert Stewart escorted Bill Parks through the corridors of the fifth floor of the five-storey building with a team of police by his side. And the police were stationed on every floor, covering every inch of the entire five-storey safehouse perimeters.

As Robert Stewart walked through the corridor headed towards the main large room where Bill Parks would remain securely guarded personally by him and the police inside, Robert could not help but experience an uneasy feeling inside of him, similar to a gnawing gut instinct, that trouble was emerging.

Robert Stewart kept this safehouse location a secret from anyone outside the New York City Police Department. In himself, Domenico Armando should not be aware of this hideout location where Bill Parks would be camped inside until his heavily armed transport team had escorted him safely out of the country for good.

But the enemy that he was dealing with was Domenico Armando. And Robert in himself had to prepare for every eventuality and safeguard against any possible attack inside the building that was premeditated by Domenico Armando even in advance.

Robert Stewart had to prepare for everything and as always, nothing ever took him by surprise.

Once Robert approached the room where Bill Parks would remain securely inside, a uniformed police officer at the door of the closed room had opened the door. It was then when Robert had that gnawing gut feeling and quickly alerted the police officer to duck towards the ground, as Robert sensed danger waiting for them inside the room.

Robert Stewart knew that Domenico Armando was determined to kill Bill Parks, and he would find a way to locate the secret safehouse where Bill Parks was currently taken to, supposedly in secret. Of course, Robert Stewart intended this hideout to remain surreptitious from everyone and everything, especially from Domenico Armando, their greatest enemy against the security of Bill Parks's life at this very moment in time.

The hideout should have remained a top-secret hiding place for Bill Parks. But sometimes things did not always go as planned. And that was exactly what Robert was trained as an expert to combat, all obstacles he would face in his profession at any given point in time!

Robert Stewart knew his enemy very well. And if Domenico Armando was determined to clip his target, he would figure out a way to find the secret location of his next target, using his extensive influence and power at his disposal, to not only identify the location, but to have his expert assassins waiting inside, somehow planted cleverly, lingering and ready for Bill Parks to show himself and blow him away, by one of those secretly planted hitmen hiding inside the building.

Robert Stewart insisted on taking the safehouse hideout stairwell as opposed to the confined possible sitting duck trap elevator. And Bill Parks and several police officers followed them up the stairs to the fifth floor. And once they entered the fifth floor, they would walk through a seeming labyrinth of corridors, until they reached the main room's location where Bill Parks would be taken inside the very extensive safehouse final destination.

As Robert Stewart told the uniformed police officer to duck onto the ground, Robert quickly grabbed for his own personal revolver concealed inside his shoulder holster inside his jacket and pointed his weapon forward at the now open door of the room where Bill Parks would be taken inside.

Captain John McCallum and Officer Paul Stewart were present to greet Robert Stewart on the fifth floor and Captain John McCallum informed Robert that they had surveillance cameras covering every entrance and exit of the extensive safehouse. The police captain also further noted that they had constant police planted inside all the monitor rooms the surveillance cameras transmitted to.

And security clearances were put in place for anyone entering the building or even exiting it for that matter.

And before anyone entered or was able to walk inside the final intended room inside the safehouse, there appeared at the open door three gunmen who fired their handgun weapons from inside the obviously not-so-secret hiding place room.

If Robert did not tell the uniformed police officer who opened the door to instantly duck, the police official would have been shot dead on the spot. There were many shots fired by the gunmen. Robert Stewart shoved Captain John McCallum to the side away from the shower of bullets coming towards them and motioned the other officers nearby to dodge the line of fire. And as soon as the firing died down, and all the police who were motioned at the side of the wall, away from the open door by Robert himself to dodge the bullets, Robert Stewart lowered himself with Paul Stewart at the scene, and both had their revolvers drawn and began firing at the three assassins and took them all out. The two policemen Robert and Paul shot them dead with two or three bullets apiece.

Once Robert and the police found that the coast was clear, without further identifiable threats witnessed in front of them, Robert, Paul and John McCallum entered the room first, to check the entire area thoroughly for anymore possible hidden threats inside, until the entire area was given an all clear. Then Robert informed the police officer guarding Bill Parks outside to summon him inside.

But that aside, Robert Stewart was extremely enraged that the security of this so-called secure safehouse, what should have been a top-secret concealed and mysterious location for all of them, was compromised.

Robert Stewart was plenty mad that Domenico Armando had managed to penetrate and infiltrate what should have been an impenetrable and safeguarded fortress. He ordered Officer Paul Stewart and Captain John McCallum that he wanted this entire safe house checked and rechecked by their teams of police for any more hidden threats of the Armando variety, that may be surreptitiously camouflaged inside.

Robert Stewart was shortly alerted that their police teams assigned to examine the entire building found several ropes tied to the metal handrails and railings of every floor of the safe house on the outside windows. And that identified the method that the Armando killers managed to enter inside the safe house, by using ropes, which assisted the hired guns in remaining undetected, via sneakily bypassing and safely detouring the security clearances posted on every traditional entrance and exit of the safe house.

Robert Stewart knew there was a leak in security. And he wanted that leak blocked. Because without a breach in their security, there would be no way the Domenico Armando goons would have been able to bypass all their security teams, even from the outside, using ropes to climb themselves on to the fifth floor of the safe house itself, to climb through the window of the identified room where Bill Parks was taken to.

Robert Stewart knew there was a very serious traitor in their midst, who knew beforehand where Bill Parks would be taken inside the safe house, as well as the location of the safe house itself.

Robert Stewart wanted that leak found, removed, blocked and punished! The police were ordered to look back at all the visual footage of the surveillance camera recordings from inside the monitoring rooms on the double, to see the identity of any possible leaks coming from inside or outside the location of the current safe house where Bill Parks was situated inside.

Robert Stewart insisted to Captain John McCallum and Officer Paul Stewart that they bring in more men, more manpower, because he wanted the entire safe house locked up tight and properly secured thoroughly with no leaks this time, and no security breaches and no infringements and violations to their safety operations.

Robert Stewart swiftly ordered forensics and the coroner to make their tracks to the safe house and identify the three dead assassins right away. It was only a short moment later when forensics identified the identities of the three assassins as hired guns for organised crime. And Robert understood that no matter what happened to those three dead assassins, Domenico Armando had an unending army supply of more assassins he could snap his fingers, in orders to come after Bill Parks with more attempts on his life. No matter how many of his terrorists were killed in the process, Domenico Armando would sanction an unending supply of hitmen after Bill Parks, until Domenico Armando was satisfied that one of those hitmen had successfully managed to slaughter the life out of Bill Parks, right in front of his archenemy rival, Police Commander Robert Stewart! **And the deed was done!**

Bill Parks was shown inside the room, and he took a seat on the leather sofa. He was slightly shocked from the apparent attempts on his life by those gunmen the police had fortunately for him, managed to outgun, before they did him in. But that aside, Bill Parks interrupted Robert's investigative discussions with his forensic officers close by and said to the Police Commander Robert Stewart, "I don't mean to be the bearer of bad news Commander, but I still believe you really haven't got a chance in hell of protecting me. No matter how good they say you are Robert, Domenico Armando is very dangerous and very determined to get me. And I fear that he might just pull it off!"

Robert Stewart did not take Bill Parks seriously at all. But he responded in a tone to humour the sorry bastard, by saying rather sarcastically, "we shall see!"

Bill Parks yet continued his smartarse commentary, "Look, Robert. I don't believe you and the New York City Police Department have a chance in preventing my inevitable demise and stopping Domenico Armando from actually successfully executing me. You boys just don't have a chance. Not a hope in hell! I'm willing to bet that I'm going to be dead before I reach that plane at New York to take me out of this country!"

Robert Stewart then stared at him dead in the eye and said firmly, "when I say that Domenico Armando will lose this war, I mean it! One way or another, you're getting out of New York. And you're going to leave the United States of America permanently. And the only way you're going to leave is the one-way Domenico Armando does not want you to leave. And that is on that private plane at New York that will fly you safely to a secret location overseas!"

Bill Parks could not help displaying panic etched on every part of his face and his eyes as he said, "I appreciate everything you are trying to do to protect me Robert Stewart, but unfortunately, I don't think prayers are going to work for me in this instance. I have committed too many evils in my life to have any prayers answered. Maybe the universe doesn't want you to protect me. Maybe the universe wants the wicked one Domenico Armando to kill me. I don't know what the truth is anymore! But anyway, good luck old buddy Commander Robert Stewart. Good luck indeed, in trying to save my miserable arse from the likes of that psychotic madman Domenico Armando! Because I know right now you are in for the fight of your life! And I'm extremely fearful that you are gonna lose this one, my old and very dear friend Commander Robert Stewart. And I think we should all be prepared for what comes next. And that is mass funerals being arranged for all our dead corpses! That's fucking inevitable!"

CHAPTER 8

Robert Stewart ordered an immediate restriction on all the facilities inside the safe house until further notice. Robert wanted the entire building, beginning with the current room where they were all situated inside with Bill Parks thoroughly investigated.

Since the breach of security was made apparent by those three hired guns witnessed inside the building earlier, Robert Stewart immediately took it upon himself to take every extra precaution necessary, in order to safeguard all their lives from possible death traps, that may be planted inside the building from top to bottom by their master criminal enemy Domenico Armando.

Robert Stewart suspected that there were elaborate and hidden lethal traps set up inside the safe house they were currently hiding inside. Robert Stewart would begin his investigation immediately!

Robert Stewart approached Captain John McCallum and asked him in silent whispers what update he had concerning the security breach inside the premises of this, no longer not-so-secret safehouse. John McCallum replied that they did a background check on the three dead organised crime Armando assassins and checked their telephone calls thoroughly, going back at least three months. John McCallum had updates concerning the telephone records of the three dead goons and their incoming and outgoing phone calls made and received. One telephone number was viewed as a single common denominator on each of their telephone records made and received by one particular New York City police officer stationed inside the building. And Robert knew that was the conclusive proof to their security violation. The officer went by the name, Elliot Archer.

Officer Elliot Archer was present with them inside the room with Bill Parks. Captain John McCallum had whispered some more important words discreetly to Commander Robert Stewart in their private corner of the room.

Captain John McCallum also had news concerning the surveillance camera devices' footage planted inside the safe house they were currently located inside. Officer Elliott Archer was spotted communicating with the three goons, prior to their deaths, outside the safe house, moments before Robert and the rest of them arrived at the compound. Officer Elliot

Archer was one of the police officers made privy to the security details and the temporary safe house location in New York where Bill Parks was to be transported to. It was Elliot Archer who telephoned the three goons to alert them of Bill Parks's arrival in due course and alerted them to be planted surreptitiously inside the room he was to be taken to, with orders to open fire and shoot-to-kill Bill Parks prior his entrance, as soon as the door was opened.

Without delay, Robert Stewart ordered the immediate arrest of Officer Elliot Archer. And before long, Elliot Archer had handcuffs placed around his wrists, as his arrest orders were carried out thoroughly, and he was taken to jail effective immediately, to deal with the repercussions of his criminal actions by the justice system.

Elliot Archer was a 40-year-old, slender-built American-descent man, with jet-black straight hair. **Now he was gone!**

Right away, like a shot - Robert Stewart went straight to business on checking the entire safe house for all hidden traps and poisons that could be planted quite cleverly, even ingeniously, by the main enemy behind all this trouble and turmoil they faced at present called, Domenico Armando.

Robert Stewart suspected that planting those three assassins inside the safe house through Elliot Archer, was just one of the methods Domenico Armando would utilise in his elaborate plots and diabolical conspiracies to murder and kill Bill Parks.

Robert Stewart suspected that since the safe house had a definite breach in its security which violated the safeties of everyone presently situated inside the building premises, that Domenico Armando would most likely plant many other hidden dangers and lethal death-inflicting traps, secretly and surreptitiously hidden throughout the entire building complex. And as a consequence, Robert Stewart was adamant to find each and every one of those extremely harmful and devastatingly dangerous hidden deathtraps, which posed a direct risk to the lives of not only Bill Parks, but the lives, the very lives of every police officer currently guarding him presently inside the safe house compound building itself. And that was why Robert restricted the use of all facilities inside the safe house, until everything was checked out thoroughly by the police and the forensic officers present inside the safe house building right now.

And so, the thorough investigation to uncover all death traps planted inside the safe house building was currently underway, effective immediately!!!

And Robert Stewart was tough and determined in his approach to make sure that no surprising skeleton and no hidden secret that could cost them all their lives, planted cunningly in the vicinity around them remained uncovered!

CHAPTER 9

As Robert Stewart and the police began searching the entire room for concealed death traps, from top to bottom, Bill Parks began revealing sordid daring details about his own shitty existence at present to Robert at the same time.

"You can't defy the odds!" Said Bill Parks seated on the leather sofa, contemplating his current dreadful fate and horrible destiny. "When a sick psychopathic crazy lunatic like Domenico Armando is gunning for you, there is absolutely no chance that you will walk out of that death sentence alive! Because I know that monster Domenico Armando. Fortunately, I don't know him personally, but I've heard enough about him to get a full picture of what he is all about! And I know he's going to get me one way or another!" Cursed Bill Parks.

The ridiculously disastrous United States of America's Health Chief continued his delivery of self-pity and idiocy, as he went on further to explain such horrendous revelations about his life's work in politics: "As US Health and Human Services Secretary, I oversaw a trillion-dollar budget. And what did I do with it? Cuts, cuts and more fucking cuts! At the same time, I cut many essential health services for the American people, I made doctors' visits expensive through the roof. And pharmaceutical prescription drugs the most expensive in the entire world. Private health insurance premiums skyrocketed, and out-of-pocket spending to the American people drove many of them broke!

"Medicare, Medicaid and the Affordable Care Act coverage was completely dismantled, and soon to all, it was bound to be vanished under my tenure, through the reshuffling and dismantling of all health portfolios across the nation under my watch! There were mass firings at the US Health Department. And massive cuts to the Health and Human Services' workforce. I legislated dramatic shifts in US health policies and vast deregulations (in terms of removing government funding), of necessary health policy priorities and initiatives, which left Americans with much fewer choices to obtain proper health care requirements for all their health care needs!

"And my recent proposals to cut Medicaid funding, which was the primary source of funding for long-term care, also significantly impacted the viability of nursing homes, which many began closing their doors, leaving seniors and the elderly in the lurch, what with reduced staffing, facility closures and horrendously decreased quality of care for the retired and the defenceless!

"NOT only that did I do, which in itself was a mortal sin as this country's health chief. But you know what I also did, Commander Robert Stewart? Don't worry. I will tell you. I also started to attack homeless people across the entire country as well. I forced the homeless to start disappearing from the streets. Homeless people began to be arrested left, right and centre all across the country. And you know why I targeted homeless people? You know why I began forcefully removing homeless people from the streets across the entire country of the United States of America? OK. OK. I know you're dying for me to answer that question, Commander Robert Stewart. So, I will tell you. Don't worry Commander. I will tell you. I began forcefully removing homeless people from the streets because as this country's health chief, I considered them to be polluting the streets!

"And that's what I did as this country's US Health and Human Services Secretary. With all the current corruption going on in the White House on both sides of politics, Democratic and Republican, this country keeps resulting in early general elections being called nationally. So, when the Republican Party won the last election three weeks ago, and as soon as I was sworn in the White House as this nation's health chief, I made rapid changes. We are now August 1998. And everyone was screaming after my changes that they wouldn't be alive to see September! I dismantled everything. I changed everything for the worse for everybody.

"I disadvantaged the poor and benefited the rich! In simple terms, I kept the health system in this country corrupt! Now when anybody tells you that politicians are liars (telling fibs before an election and doing entire reversals of their policies and election commitments once they're elected in office), you should reward and congratulate that person. Or people. Because unlike so many of us politicians - those people who are accusing us politicians of being liars are spot on. Dead on the money! They are dead right!!! And when anybody tells you that politicians are corrupt, you should also be giving that person medals for bravery! Because that individual is also correct in their assessments!

"So many of us politicians' high taxes bankrupt businesses. We are the driving force behind high inflation and corporate staffing cuts, which results in less productivity, less revenue for the nation, and ultimately an epidemic of business closures throughout the entire country, full stop! And to make up the revenue shortfall from all these businesses being liquidated, we keep raising taxes – high, high, high up to the sky! Which repeats the vicious cycle of never-ending increases in inflation and business closures, and high-to-higher levels of unemployment. Because of what us politicians are doing to this country, this nation is on the verge of exploding!

"And you know why so many politicians wanted to strip police numbers? I will also answer that question for you, Commander Robert Stewart. It is because politicians wanted to get away with their crimes without many police around to cause roadblocks to their prosperity achieved via under-the-table activities!

"And now that I've been put in this temporary protective facility here in New York, forced to resign from politics completely, before you law enforcement fellows fuck me off completely out of this country, I felt compelled to spill my guts, as if my veins were suddenly contaminated by rivers of sodium pentothal truth serum! So, in crux, to my terrible achievements as US Health and Human

Services Chief of this nation, I only benefited myself, whilst forcing the poor, the disadvantaged and the disabled to suck hind tit!"

Meanwhile, Robert Stewart was busy with forensics officers checking the water taps inside the kitchen section of the room for any signs of water supply terrorism, via acts of deliberate contamination and criminal sabotage to the water supply system throughout the entire building.

Robert Stewart was conducting a very thorough investigation concerning devilish acts committed by their specific main enemy in question, against their current location and the people situated inside it, via the implementation of chemical poisons, infrastructural tampering, and any forms of criminal sabotage, by way of biological warfare perpetrated by their opponent Domenico Armando, intended to cause immediate death to the occupants inside this safe house compound. Most specifically, the expeditious murder of this nation's Healthcare Chief, Bill Parks!

Robert Stewart poured some water into a glass from the kitchen sink tap and examined it thoroughly.

Robert lifted the glass towards his nostrils and took several sniffs of the water inside the glass. He smelled something foul. He knew the water had been poisoned. The water gave out a terribly unclean smell, that resembled bitter almonds. Robert Stewart knew the poison was most likely Cyanide. And strongly suspected the poison was Potassium Cyanide. And Potassium Cyanide was highly toxic, and it didn't take much to kill nearly any human who consumed the poison, especially through water!

Robert Stewart immediately ordered Captain John McCallum to arrange for the complete water supply driven to the safe house to be closed off. All water lines leading to the safe house he wanted switched off immediately.

Robert Stewart also conveyed specific instructions upon Officer Paul Stewart, to ensure that every police officer and security detail situated inside all floors of this safe house, maintained restriction of the compound's facilities. And especially, not to consume any water inside the premises. And to exercise extreme caution until further notice!

Robert Stewart understood quite earnestly that Domenico Armando was extremely determined to make absolutely certain that Bill Parks would not exit New York alive. And Domenico Armando was shrewd and diabolical enough to takedown any other occupant inside the safe house, who was assigned to guarding Bill Parks's life, from the evil hands and destructive clutches of the Armando Family Patriarch himself!

All in all, Robert Stewart was far from finished from his investigation inside the safe house building's premises. He suspected there were other death traps planted inside this compound's construction. And he yet proceeded to investigate thoroughly and uncover each and every one of those supposed booby traps he knew were yet hidden very cleverly inside the safe house compound facility. And it was Robert Stewart's job to examine his surroundings closely and detect and remove successfully every one of those deadly traps hidden and concealed around him!

Despite what Bill Parks thought at present, his thoughts only solidified in the fact that he was not going to exit New York City any other way except inside a body bag, Robert Stewart was still adamant and confident that Bill Parks was leaving New York and the United States of America in one piece alive this afternoon!

CHAPTER 10

Robert Stewart quickly stormed towards Bill Parks who was still seated on the leather sofa, placed two firm hands around the collar of his jacket and forced him to stand up onto his feet. At the same time he ordered him off the sofa, he instructed him to, "Stay standing up!"

As soon as Bill Parks was on his feet, Robert immediately frisked him, felt contents inside his clothing and suit blazer jacket, then told him to empty his pockets onto the wooden coffee table planted before them.

Robert Stewart studied the contents onto the wooden table after Bill Parks removed them from inside his clothing pockets. The items were standard items of keys, a wallet and some consumables. It was those consumables that Robert was most interested in examining very closely. Robert noticed that two items of consumables were a cigarette packet still fresh in its wrapper, of a Camel brand of cigarettes - and a packet of chewing gum also fresh in its wrapper.

Robert first lifted the cigarette packet and removed the plastic wrapper. Then once he opened the lid of the cigarette packet, he tilted the cigarette pack upside down and removed all the cigarettes from inside the box on to the coffee table - and began studying the residue of any possible poisons he could find inside the small cigarette box. Robert Stewart identified white powder inside the cigarette packet.

Also, Robert unwrapped the plastic off the chewing gum pack and emptied the gum onto the coffee table before him and then studied the packet enclosure of the chewing gum pieces as well. Robert also found white powder inside the chewing gum paper enclosure unsurprisingly. Furthermore, he unwrapped the paper wrapping of each individual chewing gum piece and found white powder all over the inside of each individual wrapper of the green-coloured, mint-flavoured chewing gum small items themselves.

Robert knew that the consumable items in the possession of Bill Parks had been lethally tampered with. They were violated to cause him death on the spot! And Robert could most certainly identify the type of poison used by their enemy, in order to target and kill Bill Parks as soon as he either lit a cigarette or placed any individual wrapped chewing gum piece inside his mouth.

Robert Stewart identified the poison as Strychnine. Strychnine was the poison of choice

Domenico Armando had used to obviously inject carefully inside both, the still freshly wrapped cigarette packet and chewing gum freshly wrapped packet, in order to poison and kill Bill Parks as soon as he indulged in those two various items at his leisure.

As a result of his serious findings, Robert Stewart urgently questioned Bill Parks. "When did you purchase those items and when were they delivered to you?"

Bill Parks quickly responded in between the enormous fear he felt at this moment of almost being successfully poisoned, if it had not been for Commander Robert Stewart's immediate interception of those poisons inside the consumable items in his possession. "I purchased them this morning. And they were delivered to me this morning at the Manhattan hotel. The courier left them at the security detail posted outside my hotel room, and then the security detail forwarded those items to me!"

Robert Stewart further stated, "That figures! Tell me something. That girl Foxy who was staying with you this morning at the Manhattan hotel room - when did she arrive?"

Bill Parks replied, "at about 5:00 AM in the morning. Half an hour before the cigarettes and chewing gum were delivered to me."

Robert Stewart responded emotionless, "I see. At any time that Foxy was with you, did she leave your sight for even a few moments? What I'm asking you is that were you constantly with her when she arrived at your Manhattan hotel room this morning, or was she at any time alone inside your hotel room with those cigarettes and chewing gum items of yours?"

Bill Parks understood quite clearly where Robert Stewart was heading in his line of questioning and resented the insinuation and the implication of what he was suggesting and in turn concluding. Bill Parks immediately answered the question, defending his prostitute companion that morning named Foxy, stating rather bluntly in defence of the hooker he had been screwing until the police burst inside his hotel room and interrupted his rendezvous session with her, "Foxy was with me the whole time. She was never out of my sight. She would never inject poisons into my freshly packed cigarettes or freshly wrapped chewing gum pieces. She never even had the chance. I was with her the entire time. She was never out of my sight for even one second alone with those two items in question. Besides, Foxy might be a bit rough around the edges, but she certainly is no killer being paid by Domenico Armando to inject poison in my cigarette packet and my chewing gum enclosure, to poison and kill me. She would never do such a despicable disgusting thing as murdering anybody! Please believe that Commander Robert Stewart!"

Robert Stewart replied satisfied with his answer, "OK. Then that leaves other possibilities of how Domenico Armando managed to intercept your purchases this morning and arrange for injections of deadly poisons inside those items, designed for you to consume, either by smoke inhalation or as chewing gum inside your mouth. Domenico Armando obviously could have infiltrated any number of organisations in order to arrange for those poisons to be placed inside your cigarette and chewing gum packets: the wholesaler suppliers, the retailer outlets, the courier service delivery workers. Any number of people working for those organisations could have been bribed, or in fact Domenico Armando had infiltrated, through arranging one of his cleverly disguised assassins, who could have had access at any time to those items, to in fact have them poisoned, before delivery to you this morning, for the sole purpose of murdering you. And ensuring that you never left your Manhattan hotel room alive."

Bill Parks was more than a tad shocked and startled at the revelation. "Holy shit!" He cursed. "Lucky for me, you detected those white-coloured powder poisons inside that freshly sealed cigarette packet and that freshly sealed chewing gum small enclosure, before I opened them and consumed them. And really did die as a result!"

Robert Stewart nodded his head in total agreement before saying, "you really are lucky to still be alive Mr. Bill Parks! I'm willing to bet that even if anyone of us ordered take-out food right now to be delivered here, the same Strychnine poison would be planted inside that food and drinks to be couriered at this address inside this safe house, by the very same man who tried to poison you this morning at your Manhattan hotel room. And in the case of Strychnine poisoning, either through inhalation, ingestion or absorption, first your muscles would begin to contract very quickly, and you will experience nausea and vomiting. Then muscle convulsions will lead to asphyxiation and eventual death after ingestion of that specific poison. That is one of the ways our mutual enemy planned to kill you today. And that common enemy between us is none other than Domenico Armando!"

Robert immediately bagged the poisoned items and told his forensics officers to take it to the police lab for complete and thorough analyses in its plural forms!

Within one hour, the SIA and FBI agents had arrived at the safe house to escort Bill Parks to his new safe location, to be transported overseas, destined to never return to the United States of America ever again!

Bill Parks's wife had still been in Washington, D.C. She was flown to New York hours ago to meet her husband on that awaiting plane in the city.

As Robert Stewart led Bill Parks into the hands of the SIA and FBI agents, Robert Stewart struck the palm of his hand forcefully onto the now confirmed ex-nation's healthcare chief's shoulder, jolting Mr. Parks by the powerful blow and Robert said savagely, his final parting words to him, which were: "Good Riddance!"

And as soon as Robert received official word that Bill Parks was safely taken to his secret protective custody destination abroad with his wife inside that initially awaiting New York City private plane ride, Robert Stewart then planned in his mind very strong strategic movements to combat the very ferocious and powerfully vengeful actions of Domenico

Armando, to be delivered against him expectedly, as a consequence of the Armando boss's failed results in eliminating the ex-nation's healthcare chief during this period.

Robert Stewart planned for death, and he also planned to combat death by his evil and powerful tyrant enemy named Domenico Armando! Robert Stewart certainly understood that death and destruction was coming to New York City and mostly directed at him - Robert Stewart – himself, by his enemy, the ferociously wicked, larger-than-life character, known as Domenico Armando!

Robert Stewart knew that Domenico Armando would be plenty mad and ferociously angry, particularly with him, that Bill Parks managed to escape all his death plots he had orchestrated and engineered against him this day. So, Robert Stewart prepared himself for what was to come next in the Robert Stewart and Domenico Armando War Operations against each other! Robert Stewart instinctively sensed that Domenico Armando was going to orchestrate a very diabolical scheme of payback against his number one adversary who foiled his death plots against Bill Parks this day.

So given that accurate assumption and bearing those planned vendettas in his mind by the enemy, Robert Stewart had equally planned his carefully crafted combative countermove strategies against the powerful and vindictive wrath of Domenico Armando. To end his powerful vengeful actions, destined to pour into this city thick and fast and targeted much against him, Robert Stewart himself!!!

www.ingramcontent.com/pod-product-compliance
Lightning Source LLC
Chambersburg PA
CBHW020916180626
46816CB00007BA/2433